THROUGH MY EYES

Recent Titles by Barbara Delinsky from Severn House

CARDINAL RULES
CHANCES ARE
COMMITMENTS
FAST COURTING
FIRST, BEST AND ONLY
THE FLIPSIDE OF YESTERDAY
MOMENT TO MOMENT
MONTANA MAN
SEARCH FOR A NEW DAWN
A SINGLE ROSE
SWEET EMBER
THREATS AND PROMISES
THROUGH MY EYES
A TIME TO LOVE
TWELVE ACROSS
VARIATION ON A THEME

THROUGH MY EYES

Barbara Delinsky

severn
House

This first world hardcover edition published 2015
in Great Britain and 2015 in the USA by
SEVERN HOUSE PUBLISHERS LTD of
19 Cedar Road, Sutton, Surrey, England, SM2 5DA,
by arrangement with Harlequin Books S.A.
First published 1989 in the USA in mass market format only.

British Library Cataloguing in Publication Data

Delinsky, Barbara author.
  Through my eyes.
  1. Love stories.
  I. Title
  813.6-dc23

ISBN-13: 978-0-7278-8535-7   (cased)

All Severn House titles are printed on acid-free paper.

Severn House Publishers support the Forest Stewardship Council™ [FSC™],
the leading international forest certification organisation.
All our titles that are printed on FSC certified paper carry the FSC logo.

Printed and bound in Great Britain by
TJ International, Padstow, Cornwall.

THROUGH MY EYES

1

Bad vibes. From the start, I had bad vibes about the plan. But I ignored them, because Cooper was in trouble and given all Cooper had done and been for me in the past six years, I reasoned that a small sacrifice on my part was the least I could do in return. So I swallowed my pride and called home. Cooper needed counsel, and who was more qualified to give me the name of the best criminal lawyer money could buy than my mother, the judge?

Peter Hathaway, she'd said.

I didn't recognize the name, but Mother assured me that he was the best in the business. She hadn't actually seen him in action, since she sat in Philadelphia and he practiced in New York, but she'd heard plenty about him. She sounded delighted to have an excuse to call him. That made me uneasy.

Then Dad checked him out with his friends the Humphreys who, after making their millions in pharmaceuticals, had hired Peter Hathaway to defend them against charges of falsifying research data. Lovely reference source, the Humphreys. They'd been found guilty and been heavily fined. Still, they'd praised Peter Hathaway to the hilt. That made me even more uneasy.

It didn't help matters when suddenly the whole family was involved in my affairs. I shouldn't have been surprised. It had always been that way. But I'd been removed from it for a while, so I was jolted when my brother Ian felt called upon to phone and inform me, in his own inimitably arrogant manner, that Peter Hathaway was serious legal business. Then Ian's wife, Helaine, always the vamp, added—a little too suggestively, I thought—that the lawyer was a lady-killer. My sister Samantha went so far as to say that if she divorced David, which she was seriously considering doing because he hadn't yet begun to recover the hundreds of thousands of dollars he'd lost in the stock market crash of '87, she'd go after Peter Hathaway herself. He had the Midas touch, she said.

I wondered how she knew, but I wasn't about to ask.

In any case, the endorsement was unanimous. It was the first time I could remember my family agreeing on anything—with the exception, of course, of their disapproval of my life-style—and that made me the most uneasy of all.

Peter Hathaway. He was big city, big name, big bucks—everything I'd rejected. And Cooper knew it, which was one of the reasons he was angry. He argued that Adam would never have called in reinforcements from home. Cooper may have been right. But Adam had been dead for six years. And Adam had never been charged with smuggling stolen goods.

It had been nearly a decade since I'd left what my parents considered to be civilization, but that didn't mean I was out of touch. I read the papers. I knew what Cooper would face if he was convicted. So, bad vibes or not, I hired Peter Hathaway sight unseen.

That was on Tuesday. On Friday, I steeled myself for his visit. I prepared myself for a man who was whistle smooth and arrogant, who was direct to the point of curtness and who would very likely cross-examine me even before he got to Cooper. If he *ever* got to Cooper. I hadn't yet convinced Cooper to agree to be represented.

I hadn't told Peter Hathaway that, of course. I doubt he'd have agreed to come all the way to Maine if the fact of a client had been in doubt. Then again, I'd offered him his own private, shore-front hotel for the weekend, and if that wasn't lure enough, I'd promised that a retainer would be waiting when he got here. I assumed that was adequate incentive. Still, I was going to have some explaining to do—to Peter and Cooper both.

A simple life. That was all I'd ever wanted. How things had suddenly gotten so complex, I didn't know. But then, there were lots of things I didn't know.

Like why Adam had abandoned me.

Like how Elizabeth Taylor could love my work.

Like who put a cache of stolen diamonds on Cooper's boat.

I did know how I got the headache that was building behind my eyes. I got headaches when I agonized over those things I didn't know. Adam's remedy had been a gentle forehead massage, accompanied by soothing songs sung in his soft tenor. Cooper's remedy was a dark, silent room, a comfortable bed, a warm cloth on my eyes.

Given that neither Adam nor Cooper was around, I settled for three aspirin and a cup of strong, hot tea, which I carried to the window. My front yard was looking wild and windblown, understandable since the small stone house in which I lived stood high on a bluff overlooking the ocean. I'd always found the view beyond the poor, misshapen pine to be hypnotic. Wave after wave swelled from the horizon, rolling toward the shore and imminent destruction against the rocks. I couldn't see the crash from where I stood, but its thunder was second nature to me, as was the high spray of sea foam that rose by my bluff.

I loved the ocean. Bleak as it was, particularly now that Columbus Day had come and gone, I was drawn to it. I felt at home here. I could be me. I could pull my hair into a ponytail and wear jeans and a sweater whether I was throwing clay, visiting with friends at Sam's Saloon, or waiting for a hotshot lawyer from Manhattan to arrive.

I would have glanced at my watch if I'd had one, but it had been years since I'd cared whether it was one or two or three. So I concentrated on drinking my tea with a mind toward relaxation.

All too soon the cup held little more than bits of leaves that had escaped the tea bag. They weren't much more than shadows against the porcelain; still, I studied them. I turned the cup, swirled the leaves in the few drops of tea that lingered. I imagined I saw weird configurations, shapes with no patterns, and wondered what a tea reader would say. Better still, I wondered what a psychiatrist would say. Not that it mattered. I was comfortable with myself and my life.

Tipping my head back, I swallowed the lingering drops of tea and with them any configurations of leaves, weird or otherwise. Lowering the cup, I was turning toward the kitchen when a movement at the side window caught my eye. A black car rolled to a halt on the pebbled drive. I hadn't heard a sound; the whip of the wind would have drowned it out even if it had managed to penetrate the thick, double-paned windows of the house. But then, a Jaguar would purr so softly that there would be little to hear.

Uh-huh. A Jaguar. Peter Hathaway—legal eagle, lady-killer, man with the Midas touch—would be the Jaguar type.

For a split second, every one of those bad vibes I'd experienced in the past few days belted my insides, and in that split second I felt utterly insecure. Then I caught myself, took a deep breath, looked around. This was my house, my world. I had no cause to be insecure.

Life was what you made of it. Adam and I had always believed that, and for the most part I still did. Cooper needed help; I was going to see that he got it. To do that, I had to approach this interview with confidence.

Drawing myself to my full five-foot-four even as I held the empty tea cup to my chest, I leveled a glance out the window. The first thing I noticed was that the car wasn't a Jaguar, but a more sedate-looking Saab. It was an incidental point, likely insignificant, since the car was probably a rental, but it occupied my mind for those few brief moments until its driver stepped out.

He wasn't what I'd expected at all. I'd expected a three-piece suit, not a sweater and slacks. I'd expected silver hair, not dark brown. I'd expected a slick veneer, not a rakish one.

The vibes came again, stronger than ever, setting off tremors in my stomach while the rest of me stood stock still.

I'd expected European handsome, not American handsome, but American handsome was defying the wind to stand straight and tall by his car, making a slow study of his surroundings. He looked out toward the sea; his shoulders broadened with the deep breath he took, and I could have sworn I saw a fleeting smile. More straight-faced, perhaps assessingly, he took in the front yard, its small, sad pine, the clumps of scrub grass that valiantly battled the elements. Then he looked at the house, at the roof, the fieldstone siding, the window.

Suddenly his gaze penetrated the glass and caught mine. I didn't move. It wasn't that his eyes pinned me to the spot, because if I'd wanted to leave it I could have. But I didn't want to look skittish. I didn't want to look nervous or uncertain. It seemed important that he know I wasn't afraid. It seemed important that *I* know it.

So I held his gaze until he turned and strode confidently toward the house. By the time he passed the front window, I was on my way to meet him. Confidence demanded confidence; so I'd been taught as a child, and though I'd spurned others of those childhood teachings, this one survived. Peter Hathaway barely had time to cross the small, sheltered porch

and lift a hand to knock when I opened the old oak
door.

Very slowly that hand lowered, but I was already
looking beyond it to his face. I had to look up; he
stood at least six foot two. His broad shoulders and
lean hips suggested man at his best. Nothing I saw in
his features dispelled that notion.

His hair wasn't just brown, it was a rich mahogany
and unfairly thick. Its texture appealed to the artist in
me, though it didn't take an artist to realize that the
tossing the wind had given it simply improved on the
work of a skilled stylist.

He wasn't tanned. I wasn't sure if I'd expected him
to be, and in any case, it didn't matter because his
skin had a healthy glow. It, too, was textured—
rougher where he shaved, creased where he squinted,
laughed or frowned—and there was a small scar on
his cheekbone that gave him a mysterious air.

But it was his eyes that grabbed me. They were
pale green, almost to the point of luminescence. I'd
never seen any like them. On the one hand they were
eerie, on the other enticing. They probed with an intensity that frightened me, then soothed in the next
blink. I tried to look away, but couldn't. Nor could I
control the sudden, wild beating of my heart.

"Jill Moncrieff?"

His deep voice cut through the thunder of the sea
and the echo of the wind to say my name, and I've
never been more grateful for anything in my life. For,
God help me, in those few short moments when I'd
been bound by his gaze, I'd forgotten who I was.

A single, hard swallow brought me back. "Yes,"

I said with all the composure I could muster in a matter of seconds. I extended my hand. "You must be Peter Hathaway."

His hand was large and warm, enveloping mine with the same confidence that surrounded the rest of him, but I didn't have long to dwell on it when he did something that drove all other thoughts from my mind.

He smiled.

Actually it was more of a half smile, a lopsided curve of his mouth. It held surprise, smug pleasure and utter maleness, reflecting the thoughts I assumed to be swirling through his head. It was a dangerous smile if ever there was one, but for the life of me I couldn't look away.

"So you're Judge Madigan's daughter," he announced in a soft, self-satisfied tone of voice. Still holding my hand, he made a slow sweep of my body, and while his gaze was more curious than insolent, I had to work not to squirm. He was a man with far greater experience than I possessed, and I felt vulnerable.

Reacting against that, I retrieved my hand, steadied my chin in a self-assured manner and said quietly, "That's right."

"You don't look the way I expected you would." His eyes caught mine again, this time in mild challenge.

"What had you expected?"

"A dog."

I couldn't believe he'd said that. "Excuse me?"

"I figured that being a Madigan heiress, there'd

have to be something desperately wrong with your looks for you to be stashed away up here.''

''There's nothing wrong with my looks.''

The lazy half smile came again, along with an appreciative, ''So I see.'' Then the smile faded. ''I'd also expected someone a little older. I met your brother at a party not long ago. It turned out he went to Penn with a high school buddy of mine. You must be fifteen years younger than us.''

Slowly I shook my head. ''If that was meant as a compliment, you missed. I wouldn't want to be twenty-five again for the world.''

''Why not?''

''When I was twenty-five, my husband died. My career was in limbo. I went through a rough time.'' In a chilly reminder of those dark days, the wind chose that moment to gust through the door. ''That was six years ago, Mr. Hathaway,'' I said, holding back the hair that wanted to blow into my eyes. ''I've come a long way since then. I'm quite happy with my life now, except for this little problem with Cooper.'' I stood back. ''It's chilly. Why don't you come in and let me close the door?''

I wasn't sure whether I'd shocked him with my blunt revelation about Adam. I hoped so. It bothered me that he should think me an innocent, when I wasn't. While I wouldn't call my life in Maine as sophisticated as the one I'd once known, I'd probably seen more hardship and pain—and more joy—in the past ten years than any of *my* classmates at Penn.

Keeping his feelings well to himself now, much as I would have expected from a smooth city boy, Peter

Hathaway stepped over my threshold and into the living room. Instantly the room seemed smaller than usual, which was absurd, I told myself. Cooper was every bit as tall as Peter Hathaway, perhaps even broader. When a little voice inside me whispered something about an aura of virility surrounding Peter, I tuned it out.

"Have a seat," I suggested, hoping that if his body were folded I wouldn't feel as threatened.

But he started to wander around the room, pausing before a table here, a shelf there, to study my work. "Your mother said you were a potter." He examined a pair of candlesticks that were irrevocably entwined. "She said that your things are shown in some of the best galleries in New York, but that you choose to work here for the sake of concentration."

"Mother would say that," I remarked, though not unkindly. I'd mellowed enough over the years to allow my family its excuses for what they considered to be my bizarre behavior.

"Is it untrue?" he asked. His back was to me, but I could see him touch a small vase that looked all the more delicate in contrast to his long, blunt-tipped fingers.

"To some extent. Life here is simpler than it is in the city, and in that sense it's easier to concentrate. Then again, there are many artists who work in city garrets and do just fine. Where one lives is a matter of personal choice. I've chosen to live here for reasons that have nothing to do with concentration."

He did turn then, and I half wished he hadn't. Facing him head-on, I suffered that same inner jolt that

I'd felt earlier. Something about the way he looked at me made my heart catch.

"If I asked what those reasons are," he said, "would you tell me?"

I forced myself to breathe normally. "No."

"Why not?"

"Because you're not here to talk about me. You're here to talk about Cooper."

"Then why isn't Cooper here?" he asked, with a blunt and simple logic that put me quickly on the spot—which was where, when I thought of it, I'd felt from the moment Peter Hathaway had appeared at my door.

"Cooper isn't here," I said slowly, wishing all the while that Peter Hathaway was short, fat and balding, "because I wanted to talk with you first. There are certain things you should understand before you meet Cooper."

Peter slipped both hands into the pockets of his slacks, drawing the fine gray fabric more snugly across his hips. I don't know why, but my eyes fell, then bobbed back up on a silent command, and I prayed that my face didn't look as warm as it felt.

Gesturing beseechfully toward a chair, I again urged him to sit. "Please." When he seemed determined to simply stand there, so tall and straight and beautifully masculine, looking at me, I tried a different diversion. "Did they serve you anything on the plane? Have you had lunch?"

"I didn't fly. I drove up."

That surprised me. "All the way from New York?"

"I got an early start," he explained. "I enjoy driving. I don't get to do it enough." He paused for an instant before adding, "Besides, the alternative was flying into Boston and switching to a small commuter plane. They can be harrowing. I avoid them at all costs."

Big city, big name, big bucks, afraid of flying? I had trouble believing that. If his reputation was indicative of his practice, he flew all the time. I wasn't quite sure whether he was trying to charm me into forgetting the danger of his smile by presenting me with a flaw, but if so, I wasn't buying.

"It would have been faster to fly," I told him. "I'm prepared to spend whatever it takes to clear Cooper's name. Still, the well isn't bottomless. If I'm paying you for travel time—"

"You're not," he cut in, looking around again. "If I choose to take the longer route, I cover myself. Besides, I'm not on retainer yet. I haven't agreed to take this case."

"Oh." Thanks for nothing, Mom. "I'm sorry. I was misinformed." And for that I'd offered my house for the weekend? Thanks for *nothing*, Mom.

Peter Hathaway didn't look at all disturbed. "No problem," he said and crossed to the small table that Adam and I had picked up so long ago in Nanny Walker's attic. Like most of the furniture in the room, it was a local relic. Like most, it had been stripped, sanded and restained. I loved doing things like that, loved thinking of the artisan who had originally made a piece, loved caressing the curves he or she had so painstakingly carved. After all, I was an artist, too, a partner in obsession.

This particular table was a round mahogany piece that stood on an intricately crafted pedestal and had delicate fluting around its rim. On its surface was a small, gently swirling candy dish of my own making and two photographs, each mounted in strikingly unusual metal frames made by my friend, Hans, who lived in Bangor.

Peter raised the larger of the two. It was a picture of Adam and his crew in front of the *Free Reign*. "Who's who?" he asked.

Knowing that the sooner he started learning names, the better, I crossed to where he stood and moved a light finger over the glass. "Adam...Cooper... Jack...Tonof...Benjie."

"Was that the pecking order?"

"Pretty much so. Cooper was second in command to Adam. Jack and Tonof were experienced men who worked hard but had no stake in the endeavor other than what money they earned. Benjie is Cooper's brother."

"He's just a kid."

"He was fourteen when this was taken. He's twenty now."

Peter studied the picture a little longer, then set it back on the table and lifted the smaller one. It was of Adam and me, taken during the first year of our marriage. Adam hugged me from behind in the waist-up shot. We were windblown, two blond beach bums, scantily clad, looking tanned, carefree, immortal.

"He was a handsome man," Peter commented.

"Yes."

"How did he die?"

It occurred to me to remind him a second time that he was there to discuss Cooper, not me, when I realized that, as with the identity of the crew, my answer would provide necessary background information. Besides, I had nothing to hide. Adam's death had been reported in the papers. It was matter of public record. In fact, I was surprised my mother hadn't already told him.

"There was a fishing accident. A piece of equipment went berserk. Adam was swept overboard and underwater before his crew could see, much less help."

Peter slid his gaze to me, stunning me again with its force. This time it penetrated the protective skin I'd grown following Adam's death, and for an instant, the pain was exposed, raw once more. He touched it. I would have gasped if he hadn't suddenly looked back at the photograph.

His features gave nothing away as he stood there, silently studying the picture. Only when he returned it to its place and looked at me did I realize how close we were standing. Tearing my eyes from his, I glanced down at the cold cup in my hand. "I'd like some fresh tea," I murmured and started off toward the kitchen. I thought I'd made my escape and was taking a deep, shaky breath when Peter's voice came from several paces behind.

"Any coffee?"

I swallowed the tail end of the breath and, without turning, said, "Sure."

"I'd love some, if it wouldn't be too much trouble."

"No trouble." I would have given anything to have him back in the living room, but it was too late. He was well into the kitchen. I could feel his presence through the fine hairs at the back of my neck.

Putting a hand there, I used my free hand to put the kettle on to boil, then reached for the coffee cannister.

"Neck problems?"

"No, no." Dropping my hand, I quickly measured coffee beans into the mill.

"This is charming," Peter said. I turned to find him within arm's length, looking around much as he'd done in the other room. "It has character."

Following his gaze, I took in the dovetailing of wood and tile that gave the kitchen its pecan color and its warmth. "I thought so."

"I'll bet it wasn't like this when you bought it."

Remembering that day so long ago when I'd first seen the house, I couldn't help but smile. "You bet right. It was old and ugly, the worst room in the place. We tore everything out, then put new things in piece by piece. Not that it's state of the art," I added quickly, lest he think I'd left luxury to create luxury. The kitchen wasn't luxurious, just comfortable and efficient and aesthetically pleasing. "What you see here are the basic amenities, but they're more than adequate. I can put together as elegant a meal as any situation warrants."

"Can you manage a tuna sandwich?"

That wasn't quite the kind of elegant meal I'd been picturing. "Excuse me?"

"I drove straight through," he said, immobilizing

me with those luminescent green eyes of his. "I haven't eaten since breakfast, and that was before seven this morning. If you have a can of tuna and a little mayo in the house, I'd love a sandwich. If you give me the workings, I'll make it myself. In fact," he swallowed, "give me a fork and I'll eat the tuna from the can."

I stared up at him. "You're that hungry?"

"That hungry."

"Why didn't you say so before?"

"It seemed rude. I'd just arrived."

"And the difference now?"

"This kitchen. It's very inviting."

So was he. Uncomfortably so. Looking up into those eyes, aware of the tousle of his hair, the shadow of a beard on his cheeks, the faint scent of something clean and male that clung to his skin, I felt attracted to him in ways that were strange and unbidden. After all, I loved Adam. He'd been all I'd needed when he was alive, and his memory was all I needed now.

Peter Hathaway was in my house for one reason and one reason alone—to defend Cooper. And the sooner he set about doing that, the better I'd feel.

"If you'll give me a little room," I cleared my throat and turned back to the counter, "I'll put together some lunch."

Out of the silence, I heard Peter step back, then pull a stool from beneath the adjacent counter. The stool creaked when he sat. If I'd been on the ball, I'd have taken the stool for myself, leaving him to sit a little farther off at the table. I'd have preferred that.

This way, not only could he watch everything I did, but I was aware of his doing it.

I'd missed my chance, though. Determined to ignore the large, dark form in my periphery, I focused in on my work.

"Tell me about Cooper," Peter said.

I waited until the noise of the coffee mill died, then said, "Where should I begin?"

"How long have you known him?"

"Nine years. He was one of the first people we met when we moved here."

"Why did you move here?"

"Because I wanted to pot and Adam wanted to fish."

"Was Adam's family as wealthy as yours?"

I dumped the ground coffee beans into a filter. "I thought you wanted to know about Cooper."

"I do. I'm getting there."

"A little roundabout, wouldn't you say?"

"Not really. You feel strongly enough about Cooper to bankroll his defense. If I'm to represent him well, I have to know about the people around him."

The relevance of Adam's roots to Cooper's defense was arguable; I made no attempt to hide my skepticism. But I had trouble sustaining it, trouble keeping my mind on track. Peter looked so comfortable sitting on the stool not far from my elbow that I also had trouble thinking of him as a big-shot lawyer. Big-shot lawyers didn't make themselves at home in country kitchens miles and miles from the nearest city. If it hadn't been for my mother's recommendation, I might have wondered how "big-shot" he really was.

I wondered, then, whether he read the doubt on my face, because he did turn his attention to Cooper.

"You said that he was second in command to your husband. Was he hired specifically for that purpose?"

"Yes. Adam had the boat and the desire, but he wasn't an experienced fisherman. Cooper was. It was a comfortable arrangement all around." Having poured water into the coffee maker and flipped the brew switch, I wiped my hands on the flowered towel that hung on the wall.

"Did Cooper have his own boat?"

I shook my head. "He'd always worked for other people."

"Because he couldn't afford a boat?"

"Actually," I said, moving to take a can of tuna from a side cabinet, "he could afford one. Cooper isn't a poor man. He lives modestly by choice."

The teapot began to whistle. Setting down the tuna, I turned off the gas and reached into a second cannister. Purely by chance, because there was an assortment inside, I came up with camomile tea. Camomile was calming, so they said. I needed calming, particularly when the silence lingered, for without words, Peter's presence was all the stronger. It unsettled me. Determined not to let him know, I very deliberately put the tea bag in my cup, added water from the kettle, then dipped the bag up and down, up and down, up and down. I nearly cried out in relief when his voice came again.

"So Cooper chose to work for you. I take it you liked him."

"We both did. He was quiet, but smart and hard working."

"Where was he when Adam died?"

My eyes shot to Peter's. Maybe I was being over-sensitive, but his question hit me the wrong way. The look on my face must have told him so. Almost instantly he held up a hand.

"Sorry. That sounded accusatory, but I didn't mean it that way. I'm just trying to get my bearings." He paused, then, when I didn't argue, went on. "Was Cooper on the boat when Adam died?"

Setting a mixing bowl on the counter, I said with feeling, "Yes, and he was nearly as sick as I was about the accident. There was no way he could have prevented it, still he blamed himself." I went to the refrigerator. "He and Adam were close. Cooper may not be the most demonstrative of men, but he loved Adam like a brother."

"What was his relationship to you?"

Holding the refrigerator door ajar, I thought for a minute, trying to put a word to nine years of mutual respect and genuine affection. "Brotherly," I said at last.

"Is it still that?" he asked. In the echo of his deep voice, there was no doubt as to his thoughts.

Closing the refrigerator door, I looked him in the eye. It mattered to me that Peter Hathaway know the truth, because I saw it as an important point in Cooper's favor. "If you're asking whether Cooper and I are sexually involved, the answer is no. I adore Cooper. He's been my backbone for the past six years, but there has never been anything remotely sexual about our relationship.''

"Why not?''

I frowned at his directness. "Because.''

"Not good enough. If that picture I saw was a fair representation of the two men, Cooper is even better looking than your husband. Is he already married?''

"No.''

"Gay?''

"No!''

"How do you know?''

"Because he has women to satisfy the urge when he gets it.''

"How do you know?''

Because Swansy told me, though how Swansy knew was a mystery, but Swansy was never wrong. "I know. Trust me. I know.''

"And he's never made a pass at you.''

I stared at him for a minute, making no attempt to hide my annoyance. "Why does sex have to be involved?''

"Because you're no slouch.''

"What does *that* have to do with anything?''

His voice was low. "Two attractive, unattached people in a secluded place, a place where winters are made for sharing the heat of a lover?'' His eyes seemed suddenly darker. "If I were in Cooper's shoes, I'd have made a pass at you.''

I felt that little heart-catch again and ignored it, just as I refused to acknowledge his claim. "But why does it matter?'' I asked more quickly than I might have if I'd been perfectly calm. "What does it have to do with Cooper's case?"

Peter was watching me closely. "I'm just trying to figure out what you two mean to each other."

"We're the best of friends. The very best. But that's all."

He eyed me cautiously. "Are you sure?"

"Very."

For a minute longer, he studied me. Though his eyes never left my face, they seemed to take in far more than mere features. They delved into me, touching things that were deep and private and had to do with Adam and me, more so than with Cooper. They asked questions, probed territory that had been untouched for years.

I didn't understand it. I'd met many people, made many friends in the past six years, yet none had ever gotten to me this way. It frightened me that Peter Hathaway should. He was a total stranger. But powerful, so powerful. Beneath his gaze, I felt bared.

Pulling the refrigerator door open, I ducked inside. When I emerged, my arms were filled with a jar of mayonnaise, a head of lettuce and a loaf of bread. It wasn't that I believed they could shield me from his gaze, but I had to try something.

As it happened, by the time I straightened, Peter was looking out the window. I followed his gaze, thinking maybe Cooper was coming. He'd promised me that he would, though I'd had to work hard for that promise.

I could have used his help right about then. But there was no sign of him on the walk.

"Where does he live?" Peter asked.

I set to work mixing the tuna. "In town. It's five minutes by car, fifteen by foot."

"Does he live alone?"

"No. Benjie lives with him."

"Any other relatives?"

"There used to be," I told him, keeping my eyes on my work. "Cooper's lived here all his life. His father died when he was seven or eight. He had a sister, but she left when their mother remarried." I took a breath. "Benjie is actually Cooper's half brother, the son of his mother and her second husband."

"Where are they?"

"His mother and stepfather? Dead."

"Both of them?"

"Yes. There was a fire one night. Neither of them made it out of the house."

"When was this?"

"About a year before Adam and I moved here."

"Where was Cooper at the time?"

My fork snagged in the tuna. Slowly I looked up. "Cooper was working on a boat two days north of here. It took the Coast Guard that long to reach him. No, he didn't have anything to do with that fire. Arthur managed it all by himself."

Rather than trying to catch Cooper in something, Peter seemed totally engrossed in the tale. "Arthur?"

"Cooper's stepfather. He was an alcoholic. When he wasn't drinking, he was abusing Cooper's mother. He'd done both on the night of the fire. According to the medical examiner, MayJean was unconscious when the fire started.''

''How did it start?''

''He was smoking. Fell asleep. He couldn't get himself out any more than he could get her out.''

''And Benjie?''

''Thank God, Cooper had sent him to stay with a friend. He often did that when he had to be away for more than a day or two. Arthur had been known to take his ugliness out on Benjie, too.''

Peter frowned. ''How could Cooper stand by and let that happen?''

I was taken aback by his criticism, which was rash and unfounded. ''What could he do?'' I asked angrily. ''He argued with his mother until he was blue in the face, trying to get her to bring charges against Arthur, but she wouldn't. And she wouldn't leave him. So there wasn't much of a case. The best Cooper could do was to try to keep Benjie out of the line of fire.'' I went back to mixing the tuna with greater force. ''Cooper's life hasn't been easy. I've always admired his fortitude in the face of that.''

Peter was quiet. I dared a glance at him. He looked pensive as he stared out the window, but I didn't have time to wonder why before he grew alert and met my gaze. ''I take it Cooper took over the fishing business when Adam died.''

Satisfied that I'd successfully defended Cooper on the matter of his family, I felt comfortable moving on. ''That's right.''

''Do you still own the boat?''

"No. I deeded it to Cooper three years ago. It took me that long to get him to take it."

"Strange."

"Not if you know Cooper. He's as loyal a person as I've ever met. Running the boat for me meant as much to him as running it for himself. He simply didn't aspire to more." I reached for the loaf of bread. "Which is what makes these charges against him so absurd. Cooper Drake doesn't want or need money, so there's no motive. Aside from a speeding ticket or two, he hasn't broken a law in his life. He picks and chooses his friends with care, and he doesn't mix with thugs. There is no way he had anything to do with the smuggling of those diamonds."

"They were found on his boat. In his cabin. In a laundry bag with his name stenciled on it."

My heart beat faster. "You've talked with someone."

He nodded. "Assistant U.S. Attorney Hummel. We have a mutual friend in New York. When I told him I'd been asked to take the case, he filled me in one what's happened so far."

And that, I supposed, was why I was willing to overlook the bad vibes I'd had. A lawyer with clout could get things done. It was as simple as that.

"How is the State's case?" I asked cautiously.

Peter shrugged with his mouth. "Not great. At least, based on what he told me, it's not."

"But Cooper was caught with the diamonds. Isn't possession nine-tenths of a conviction?"

"All it takes is one-tenth to establish reasonable

doubt, and with reasonable doubt comes an acquittal.''

''Do you think you can get one?''

''If I can establish reasonable doubt.''

''Do you think you can?''

''I won't know until I've spoken with Cooper.''

''But you will take the case.''

''Again, I won't know until I've spoken with Cooper.''

All roads led to Cooper. I was beginning to feel uneasy. ''Why is that?''

''Because I have to get a feel for the man. I can't represent him unless I believe in him. And if it turns out that he and I don't see eye to eye on what has to be done—'' He made a ''pfft'' sound and tossed his head.

With deliberate care, I took two slices of bread from the package, put them on a plate, covered one with tuna, then lettuce, then set the other on top. I made a neat diagonal cut in the finished product and set the plate before Peter. Instantly he began to eat, which was just what I'd hoped he'd do. Hungry and mean was fine for the trial; for now, I needed full and indulgent.

Crossing my hands on the counter, I said, ''By definition, a criminal lawyer defends criminals—''

He interrupted me with a raised finger, held it there until he'd swallowed, then said, ''Alleged criminals.''

''Alleged criminals. Some of whom are totally innocent. They must be angry at having been accused. You must bear the brunt of their anger sometimes.''

''Sometimes.''

I thought for a minute, choosing my words with care. ''There must be times when a client sees you as part of the system and resents you for that.''

Having taken another mouthful, he gave a slow, silent nod.

''And times,'' I went on, ''when a client doesn't want help from anyone, least of all you.''

Peter stopped eating and gave the smallest tilt to his head. ''Are you trying to tell me something, Jill?''

''Tell you something?'' I asked. My voice was a little higher than usual. I wasn't sure whether it was because he saw too much too fast, or whether it was simply the way he said my name. In either case, I was in trouble.

''Is Cooper angry?''

I debated lying, but it seemed pointless. ''Yes.''

''Is he resisting help?''

''Would you like milk with this, or just coffee?''

''Jill?''

I felt a flicker of annoyance. ''Yes, he's resisting.''

''Does he know I'm here?''

''Of course, he knows you're here. I wouldn't have dragged you all the way from New York without mentioning it to him.''

Looking thoughtful, Peter popped the last of the sandwich half into his mouth. When it was gone, he speared me with an accusatory gaze. ''You mentioned that I was coming, but he hasn't agreed to cooperate.''

''He's upset. He doesn't understand the difference a good lawyer can make.''

''Did he agree to talk with me?''

''Yes.''

"Is he coming over here?"

"Yes."

"When?"

"Sometime this afternoon. I couldn't pin him down to a time. But he promised he'd be here."

Without another word, Peter started eating again. When he'd finished his first sandwich, he reached over, removed another two slices of bread from the loaf, forked up some of the tuna left in the bowl and made a second sandwich. Swiveling in the other direction, he pulled the refrigerator open. He had to leave the stool to get at the milk, and before I had time to prepare myself, he was standing beside me, looking for a glass.

Again I felt that tiny catch in my chest. It was hard to ignore this time because it made my hand shake when I opened the cabinet. I made a vague gesture that he should help himself and quickly lowered my hand to the solidity of the counter. He took the glass, but didn't move away. Nor did he say a word.

Barely a hair's breadth separated us. My shoulder was an inhalation away from his chest, my arm his middle, my hip his groin. He was close enough for me to feel the soft movement of his breath in my hair and smell the wonderfully male scent that had taunted me earlier. But it was the heat of his body that affected me most; it penetrated both his clothing and mine to tempt me with the kind of solace that I'd been without for six long years.

Move, I told myself, but I couldn't budge. The message of my mind couldn't reach my legs because of the swelling of all kinds of sensations in between. So

I stood there helplessly, feeling the lure, the attraction, the desire. My breath came shallowly, working around my hammering heart as I stared at the tiled countertop and waited for him to speak. When I felt my body begin to list that smallest, smallest bit into his heat, I knew I could wait no longer. I had to break the spell, because that was what it was, I was sure of it. Peter Hathaway had put me under a spell. I wasn't normally affected by men this way. I just wasn't.

"Peter?" I said in a voice that was barely more than a whisper.

"Hmm?"

It wasn't a mischievous "hmm" or a mocking one or even a seductive one. It was a very quiet "hmm" that was so innocent, so thoughtful that it was indeed sexy.

Distracted by the idea of sexy, I started again. "Peter?"

"Yes?"

There was something I wanted to tell him but the words weren't coming. "I, uh…" It had to do with Cooper. I struggled, dug deep for the thoughts. "There are several things you should understand…before he gets here."

For another minute, Peter didn't move. Then, slowly, he stepped away from me. Without caring how it would look, I hung my head and took in the deep breath my lungs craved. When I raised my head and glanced over at him, his back was to me. He was pouring milk into the glass that had brought him so close to me in the first place.

At first glance he looked perfectly calm, totally unaffected by what had just shaken me to the bone. Then I noted that his shoulders were very straight, and his head remained bowed well after he'd finished pouring the milk.

Something had touched him, too. I wasn't sure what it was, wasn't sure whether he found it as unwelcome as I did, but knowing that I wasn't the only one with a problem made me feel better.

Taking advantage of his momentary distraction, which gave me the only edge I might have in a while, I addressed what I told myself were the first of my priorities. "There are several things you have to understand about this case," I said quietly. "The first is that your bills are to be sent to me. I don't want any mention of money in front of Cooper. The second is that I want the best defense possible. If you can get the case dropped before it goes to trial, so much the better, but in any case, I want Cooper exonerated. And the third," I said, "is that I don't care how reluctant Cooper is, I want you as his lawyer."

Peter looked past his shoulder at me. "Are you sure?" he asked cautiously, and I knew he was thinking of what had just happened.

So was I. But I was also thinking that I was in control. I couldn't deny that Peter Hathaway turned me on, but I sure as hell could overcome it. After all, I had the strength of Adam's love on my side.

"I'm sure," I said. "I think you're just the man to defend Cooper."

"Why?"

I supposed I could say that he seemed bright and articulate, honest and dedicated, and all of that was true, but the thing that stuck out most in my mind was the picture he and Cooper would make in the courtroom. Between them, they'd knock the socks off any females who happened to sit on the jury.

Not wanting to tell Peter that, I said, "Because my mother says you're the toughest and the best. I trust her judgment."

After a long, expectant silence, Peter said, "I accept that."

Something in his tone made my eyes widen. "You'll take the case?"

"I'll take the case."

I hadn't expected the turnaround. "But you haven't met Cooper. You said it would depend on—"

"I know what I said, but I've changed my mind."

"Why?"

"Because you intrigue me."

My mouth fell open. "That's a *lousy* reason for accepting a case."

"Not really." His eyes held mine as he came closer. "Between you and your mom and Hummel, I've learned enough about the case to know that it'll be a challenge. If Cooper and you are best friends, he can't be all that bad. I need a break from the city. This is perfect. You've offered me your hospitality. And you're here." He paused, then said in a husky tone, "This case is just what I need."

I didn't like the tone any more than I liked the look in his eyes. It was hungry—hungry in the way of a man who knew how to satisfy a woman and satisfy her well, hungry for the kinds of things I'd sworn I'd never give again.

Hunger alone I could resist, but there was a gentleness there, too, that posed a far greater threat. I was a sucker for gentle men. Adam had been one. So, in his dark way, was Cooper—who, praise be, chose that moment to walk through the kitchen door.

Looking disgruntled, he stared first at me, then at Peter. In the silence that ensued, I had the uncanny notion that it was my future, not Cooper's, that hung in the balance.

Without leaving my side, Peter extended his hand. Cooper eyed it, eyed me, eyed Peter. I held my breath, unsettled as I'd never been, because though Peter would be the best thing for Cooper, he might well be the worst thing for me.

Then Cooper's hand slowly went out, and I was trapped.

2

———————

From my perch on the stool, I silently watched the two men at the table. Though they'd asked me to join them, I'd declined. It seemed important that they establish a relationship without my interference. At least, that was the excuse I gave myself, though if I'd truly wanted to give them privacy, I'd have left the room.

I didn't do that for two reasons. First, I wanted to make sure Cooper cooperated. And second, I wanted to see how Peter Hathaway worked.

Sitting on the stool by the counter gave me spectator status. It also removed me just a bit from Peter, which meant that I could relax some. Cooper's presence helped; he was my ally, loyal, devoted, steadfast. He was also in a lousy mood. Yes, he'd come, but he was looking tired and taut. He participated in the meeting only to the extent of answering the questions Peter asked. He didn't volunteer a thing.

I had to hand it to Peter. Undaunted by Cooper's reluctance, he posed question after question, each in the low, even tone that reminded me of what Ian had said. "Serious legal business," he'd attributed to Peter, and I could see it. There were no grins, no editorial comments, no questions that didn't have direct relevance to the case. He read Cooper well. Perhaps he'd had experience with dozens of Coopers, but he understood that this one needed a low-keyed, meat-and-potatoes approach. That was one of the reasons I assumed he made notes by hand on a yellow legal pad, rather than using the small recorder I'd seen in the briefcase he'd brought in from the car.

Since I was familiar with the facts of the case, I listened to the discussion with only half an ear. I already knew that the *Free Reign* had been on a two-week trip fishing off the shores of Newfoundland, that she'd stopped at Grand Bank for supplies midway through, that she'd returned to Maine right on schedule. There had been nothing new about the itinerary; Cooper had followed it dozens of times before. This time, though, U.S. Customs agents had been waiting to welcome him home.

Without making a big deal of it, Peter asked, "Did you know anything about those diamonds?"

"No," Cooper answered.

"You had no idea they were on the boat?"

"None."

"They were found in your cabin. If you don't know how they got there, maybe one of your crew does. Any suggestions?"

"No. My men are all honest and hardworking."

"Are any of them financially strapped?"

"They all are. If they weren't, they wouldn't be in this line of work. It's hard."

"Forget strapped. Talk panicked. Are any of them in the midst of serious financial crises?"

"All the time," Cooper said with a cynical twist to his lips.

I wanted to shake him. He knew what Peter was getting at, but he was being difficult. At that moment, I admired Peter his patience. Though he spoke a little slower than normal when he rephrased the question, he made it sound more pensive than tempering.

"Has any of your crew suffered any recent out-of-the-ordinary financial crisis?"

"Not that I know of."

"Would you know?"

"Probably."

Peter made several notes on his pad. I couldn't read them from where I sat, but I could watch the movement of his head. He held the pen oddly, as though awkward with it, and though he wrote quickly enough, I wondered what kind of student he'd been in school.

Brilliant, no doubt. I wondered why I'd wondered in the first place.

Drawing several broad lines across the page, he began to ask Cooper questions about individual members of the crew. While my half-an-ear continued to listen, the rest of me strayed.

I'd guessed right; Peter and Cooper were a handsome team. Both were tall, each imposing in his way. Cooper, wearing T-shirt, flannel shirt and jeans, clearly was the rougher-edged of the two. His hair was darker, the stubble on his cheeks darker, his eyes darker. I wanted to blame the grimness of his expression on the situation, but the fact was that Cooper had a shadowed side not even I had touched in nine years of trying. I'd long since learned that parts of Cooper were off-limits; but then, parts of me were, too. Cooper and I accepted that about each other, which was one of the things that made our relationship work.

Peter, on the other hand, wasn't so much dark as new and, therefore, an enigma. Whereas I could guess that Cooper was feeling frustrated and constrained and angry as hell at the situation and all those related to it, Peter's feelings escaped me. I supposed it was to be expected. I didn't know the man. His features were controlled. Little slipped past his professional facade.

Oh, I could guess things. I could guess that he found me attractive. I intrigued him, he said. And I wasn't so ignorant as to think he was fascinated by my mind. He was male through and through. I was willing to wager that his sexual prowess rivaled his legal skill. Whether wandering through my living room, standing by my counter or sitting in one of the ladder-back chairs at my table, his lines flowed. He was comfortable with his body; he handled it well.

I supposed others had handled it well, too, over the years.

But I wasn't entirely sure. Helaine had called him a lady-killer, but what did Helaine know? Rumor had a way of feeding upon itself, particularly where sex was involved. Perhaps rumor was wrong. Perhaps Peter Hathaway was the monogamous type. Perhaps he'd been married and divorced, or engaged and burned. Perhaps he had a long-time steady lover in Manhattan. Or he'd sworn off women completely. Or he was hung up on his mother.

His love life was one big, fat question mark. Even the half smile he'd given me, the one that had set my equilibrium back so, had been mysterious in its way, as though it held a secret that I ought to know but didn't.

"Hutter Johns wouldn't have done anything like that," Cooper barked, intruding on my thoughts, retraining them on the discussion at hand. "Yes, he's the newest member of my crew, but he's one of the most open."

"Sometimes the open ones are the most deceptive," Peter returned. "They toss out red herrings right and left."

"Not Hutter," Cooper vowed. "Not to me." He clamped his mouth shut.

Reaching quickly for the coffeepot, I skirted the table and went to his side. When I put a tentative hand on his shoulder, his gaze flew to mine in surprise— as though he'd momentarily forgotten I was in the room—and then softened in the subtle way that was characteristically Cooper. I refilled his mug, then moved around and did the same for Peter. Once I'd replaced the glass carafe on its warmer, I returned to Cooper's side.

Peter looked up from his mug. If he thought anything of my change of position, he didn't let on, and it certainly didn't deter him from his purpose. He'd apparently reached the point where he felt a little pushing was in order. Though his voice was quiet, his eyes were clear and sharp. "If neither you nor your crew had anything to do with the smuggling of those diamonds, how did they get onto the boat and into your cabin?''

Stone-voiced, Cooper said, ''I don't know.''

''You must have a theory.''

''I assume they were put on the boat while we were docked at Grand Bank.''

''By whom?''

''If I knew that, I wouldn't be sitting here now.''

''Where would you be?''

''Fishing.''

More softly than Cooper, I told Peter, ''The boat's been impounded, and the crew is filing for unemployment. It isn't a great situation.''

Peter's gaze caught mine, and I imagined I saw a germ of compassion there before he turned back to Cooper. ''Why would someone have picked the *Free Reign*?''

''Because,'' Copper said without pause, ''we're predictable. And reliable. We leave here on schedule, we come back on schedule. And we're above reproach.''

''Until now.''

Cooper didn't respond. Since I stood slightly behind his shoulder, I couldn't see his face, still I knew without a doubt that it was granite hard. I could feel his anger, a tangible thing very much in control of his being, and I had the uncomfortable notion that he was getting ready to bolt. That was the last thing I wanted. So I spoke up in his defense.

''Cooper is innocent. In the nine years I've known him, he's never done anything even remotely questionable. He keeps detailed records of where he's fished and what he's caught. The fishing authorities trust him. I trust him. He's innocent. So is the *Free Reign*. They've been used, that's all. We have to find out by whom.''

''How do you propose we do that?'' Peter asked.

''I was going to ask you the same question.''

He took a slow swallow of his coffee, set the mug down and leaned back in his seat. ''I could talk with the police, but obviously they feel they already have their man. I will plant some doubt. That won't hurt, and I can do it easily enough, but a little doubt won't spark an active investigation.'' He looked from Cooper's face to mine, then back. ''We could conduct one ourselves. We could hire an investigator. But it'll cost.''

''No,'' Cooper said. ''No investigator.''

Tightening my hand on his shoulder, I said to Peter, ''We'll think about it. In the meantime, what can we do?''

His answer was on the tip of his tongue. ''Talk with people, anyone and everyone around here who has anything to do with Cooper or the boat. The crew comes first. I want to talk with each of them.''

Feeling the tension coil tighter in Cooper's shoulder, I leaned forward. ''It has to be,'' I told him in a private voice, ''if for no other reason than to line up witnesses who'll speak on your behalf.''

Staring at me, he spoke nearly as quietly as I had, albeit rigidly. ''I didn't want this.''

''What was the alternative?''

''McHenry.''

''McHenry couldn't have done it.'' I sighed. ''Cooper, we've been through this before. McHenry got you out on bail in twice the time it should have taken. He would defend you, and you're right, he wouldn't ask any questions or make any waves, but neither would he get you an acquittal and that's what you need. The alternative, Cooper, is jail.''

''I know that,'' he growled, but I wasn't done. Once started, I had trouble stopping.

''You've worked too hard. You've worked too hard to make a life for yourself. And for Benjie—if you go to prison, where will that leave him? Where will it leave *me*?'' I looked at Peter. ''Reasonable doubt. That's all we have to show. Reasonable doubt.'' The phone rang. Ignoring it, I told Cooper, ''Peter can do it, but it won't be easy. You have to cooperate. We'll all have to cooperate.''

''I'm missing out on good fishing.''

''I'm missing out on good potting, but this is more important than either of those things. It's your *life*, Cooper.''

''What's it worth?'' he muttered.

The phone rang again.

''A whole lot, damn it,'' I cried in an angry whisper, ''at least, that's what you told me after Adam died, when I didn't care what happened to me. Or was it a line? Were you lying?'' I'd reached him. He was looking at me with the kind of dark awareness I knew so well. ''Peter knows what he's doing. All we have to do is to cooperate with him. I'm asking you, *begging* you to do that.''

''He's expensive, Jill.''

The phone rang again.

"It's my money. What else am I going to do with it?"

"Buy a condo in the city."

"What?"

"You heard."

I was sorry I had. "I don't want a condo, and I don't want the city!"

"Not now. Maybe in a year or two."

"Never."

"It's getting time, Jill."

"Never!" The phone rang again. Swearing, I crossed the room and snatched it up. "Hello!"

"Jill?"

Hanging my head, I took a minute to compose myself. Then I said brightly, "Hi, Samantha."

"Is he there?"

"Who?" I asked, as if I didn't know.

"Peter."

"Oh." I looked at the floor. "Uh-huh."

"Is he gorgeous?" she asked. I could just see her eyes. They'd be wide and as eager as her grin.

I turned my back on the two in the room. "How's David?"

Samantha ignored my pointed question, which was nothing new. She was my older sister by seven years and had always seen me more as a nuisance than a friend. Of course that didn't mean she couldn't seek me out when it suited her purpose. Now was one of those times.

"I've never met Peter," she said in a breezy tone that was a little too intent to be casual. "It's only in the past five years that he's made a name for himself.

Supposedly he went to law school late, and what he did before that is a big mystery. Is he as handsome as he looks in the papers?''

I heard the murmur of voices behind me. ''I can't talk now, Samantha.''

''He sitting right there? Oh, Lord. And Mom says you have him for the weekend. You are one lucky woman. Then again, you probably don't realize it. Or you're a nervous wreck. You haven't dated since Adam died, have you?''

Stretching the cord, I moved into the hall, put a shoulder to the wall and my back to the kitchen and spoke into the receiver, which was practically touching my lips, ''I don't know what you're talking about. This is a business meeting.''

''It may start out as one, but it doesn't have to end that way.'' Her voice dropped with conspiratorial urgency. ''Listen to me, Jill. Peter Hathaway is a catch. He'd be good for you and good for us. We need new blood in this family, and I can't think of better blood than his. He's successful, he's loaded and he's available. You have him for the weekend. *Go* for it.''

I didn't want to be listening to that, when far more important things were being said in the kitchen. ''I can't talk now. *Really*, Samantha.''

I'd tried to keep the words as soft as possible, but my impatience must have shown. Samantha's corresponding pique came through loud and clear.

''You don't want to talk. You *never* want to talk, because you think you know it all. Well, you don't, Jill. You don't know anything about men. You dated Adam from day one at Penn. You married him. You went off to live in the wilds. Then he died on you, and you've lived the life of a nun ever since. Is that what you want for the rest of your life?''

''For God's sake!'' I cried, then, remembering the men not far away, lowered my voice to a rough whisper. ''What's with you?'' Back to the wall, I slid down until my bottom hit the floor. ''You're trying to make something out of absolutely nothing!'' Turning away from the kitchen, I tucked myself up to prevent my voice from carrying far. ''My best friend is in need of legal assistance. I'm seeing that he gets it. This is business. That's all. Business. Period.''

In the silence that followed, I turned my head and tried to tune in to what was being said behind me, but the words were low and indistinct. Then Samantha's voice came more stridently, and I gave up trying.

''Business, period? What about broadening yourself? Hmm? I thought you were interested in doing that. You moved to the boondocks to be closer to nature. You said you wanted to broaden yourself artistically. Well, what about socially? Or romantically? This is your chance, Jill. Don't blow it!''

Against my will, my temper rose. ''My chance for what? To have a wild and sexy weekend? If that's your definition of exciting, or broadening, fine. But don't impose it on me. I have better ways to spend my time.''

''Sure you do—playing the martyr. You've been doing it so long, you don't know anything else.''

''Shut up, Sam.''

''You're such a pill. Either that or you're totally

ignorant. If I didn't have other plans, I'd fly up there and show you how it's done. Obviously you have no idea how to seduce a man.''

It had hurt when she'd called me a martyr, but I could rationalize that when it came to my feelings for Adam, she didn't know what she was talking about. When it came to sex, though, she did, so her insult stung. I'd grown up being put down, feeling inadequate in comparison to Samantha, but I was no longer a child. I didn't have to stand for her abuse.

Angrily sitting straighter, I said, ''If that's what you think, Samantha, then you're the one who's ignorant. I haven't led as sheltered a life as you'd like to believe. There are some stunning men up here, and I mean stunning. They don't have designer clothes and cars and condos to fall back on, so they have to produce the appeal all by themselves, and they do it well. They have what's called unfettered virility. They're sexy as hell. I could seduce a man like that in a minute.''

''But have you?'' Samantha hummed smugly.

''Wouldn't you like to know?'' I hummed back just as smugly.

She paused for the space of a breath before offering an arch, ''Excu-se me. I thought I might be of some help. Obviously you don't need it. Have a good weekend.''

Seconds later I found myself holding a dead receiver. Pressing the end of it to my mouth, I felt an old, familiar sadness steal through me. I'd accepted the fact that Samantha and I would never be close, and it wasn't just her fault. I was, in many ways, nearly as headstrong as she, so I shared the blame. But I was sorry. There had been times over the years when I could have used a sister.

Taking a deep breath, I swiveled on my bottom in a prelude to standing, only to come face to face with a long pair of legs. I cried out in alarm. My gaze shot upward, over narrow hips, a lean middle, then wider shoulders to Peter's complacent face.

''My Lord, you scared me,'' I breathed, pressing a hand—with its telephone receiver—to my pounding heart. ''I'm so used to being alone. I'd forgotten anyone was here.'' But remembrance came fast. I glanced past him and grew uneasy. ''Where's Cooper?''

''He left.''

''Oh no,'' I wailed softly.

''No sweat. We're meeting again tomorrow afternoon.''

I sank back against the wall in relief. For an instant, I'd imagined that Cooper had taken advantage of my absence to storm off. If he'd done that, I'd have been furious with him, and with Samantha for having distracted me, and with myself for having been distracted.

And I had definitely been distracted. I'd completely forgotten about the men nearby. Looking off in the opposite direction from where Peter stood, I tried to think of what I'd said at the end of my conversation with Samantha that he might have overheard. One possibility was as bad as the next.

And Peter simply gazed down at me, not letting on what he'd heard, leaving me to wonder.

I raised my eyes to his, then dropped them back to

the floor. Along the way, I had a second viewing of his length. It was impressive. He was a large man, long and lean. Beneath him, I felt small.

Delicate.

Feminine.

Get up, I told myself, but I couldn't budge. My legs felt like rubber, and no wonder. The blood that was normally there had been rerouted to my chest. At least, it felt that way, my heart was thudding so loudly.

Nearly frantic to fill the silence between us with some sort of diversion, I looked up at Peter and said, ''So. What do you think of Cooper?''

He didn't answer at first. He had a shoulder propped against the wall and looked as if he could stay that way for a while. I was glad one of us was comfortable.

''I'm not sure,'' he answered at last. ''He's tense. And angry.''

''I told you he would be. But do you think you can work with him?''

Again he didn't immediately answer, and this time I wondered if the pause was for my benefit. With each minute that passed, I grew more aware of the way he dominated the narrow hall. ''Mastery'' was the word that came to mind. Peter Hathaway was definitely in control.

''I can work with him,'' he said.

I was grateful for small favors. ''Good.''

''Not that it'll be easy. He doesn't trust me.''

''Only because you're new. But distrust is the least of Cooper's worries.'' With the directing of my thoughts to something constructive, I found the strength to stand. Not to move away, though. I figured I'd take it step by step. "It's the whole situation," I said, trying to explain. I leaned against the wall, hugging the telephone to my chest. "He's furious with it. If he had his way, good old Chad McHenry would wave his hands and say a few words to the judge and the whole thing would be over and forgotten. But that won't happen and, deep inside, Cooper knows it. Deep inside, he knows you're his best hope. But it's like exercising, you know? No pain, no gain. Trouble is he's already in pain. He doesn't relish the thought of more."

"Why will it be so painful for him if I talk with people in town?" His voice seemed softer, more intimate now that my face was closer.

I took a shallow breath. "Because he's a private—and prideful—man. He doesn't like the idea of other people talking about him, and I can't blame him for that. It's a disconcerting feeling."

"You've had personal experience?"

"Oh, yeah." I thought of all the family gatherings I'd absented myself from where the topic of conversation had no doubt been my self-imposed exile. And then there was Adam's death. "For months after the accident, I'd walk down a street and wonder who was watching from which window feeling sorry for me. I didn't want pity. Neither does Cooper."

"I'm not looking for pity. I'm looking for information. I want to know what people around here think about what's happened and why."

"They're apt to be wary, just like Cooper was," I warned. "You're a stranger."

"But you'll be with me," he said calmly.

I blinked. "I will?"

"You're my entrée."

I hadn't counted on that. I'd assumed that Peter would talk with Cooper, then go about his business on his own. I was paying the bills and throwing in room and board. I hadn't expected to be an assistant to the attorney, as well.

"This weekend?" I asked in a thin voice.

Peter nodded.

"Uh, I don't know if I can handle that." In more ways than one. "I've pretty much booked up my time."

"With something wild and sexy?"

My pulse tripped. He'd heard what I'd said. Then again, maybe he hadn't. Maybe he was just trying to be cute. "Actually I have work to do. I have a show coming up in a month. My sales representative wants to have a dozen new pieces by then. I've only got four done."

Peter gave that some thought, but when I expected him to come up with something as cute as "wild and sexy," he asked instead, "Where is the show?"

"New York."

"Ah. Then you'll be coming to the city."

"I haven't decided yet." There was no harm in telling the truth. "I don't really love going to those things. Moni—that's the woman who handles my work—says I have to be there, but I missed the last one and it didn't hurt sales."

"Why don't you like shows?"

"I don't know." I looked down at the phone which I held more loosely now against my chest. "Maybe I've gotten un-used to big crowds and wearing high heels and nursing drinks that I didn't want in the first place."

His voice came lower, closer. "Art shows are notorious for stunning men."

Once I could chalk up to coincidence. Not twice. He'd definitely heard what I'd said to Samantha. Looking up, I found his eyes no more than a foot away from mine. I searched them, looking for the taunting I was sure I'd heard, and indeed, hidden in their luminescent green depths was a flicker of amusement, but just a flicker. There was also a whole lot of curiosity.

It was the curiosity that started the quivers inside me this time, because it was honest and genuine and very serious. There were things about me that had Peter Hathaway guessing.

There were parts of me that liked it that way.

I made light of his remark. "Stunning men are a dime a dozen in New York. If they want to be seen, it's either there or L.A."

"Or here."

It struck me then that he wanted to discuss what he'd overheard. I knew I could put him off, but I wasn't sure it was worth the effort. "Okay. You heard what I said to Samantha."

He didn't try to deny it. "You're right. City men often do depend on material things to enhance their virility. Maybe they feel that's the only way they'll be noticed among the hordes. Everywhere they turn, they face competition. They lead congested lives. Sometimes the raw basics are forgotten.''

''They? Don't you consider yourself one of them?''

He gave a slow, almost somnolent shake of his head, and though his eyes were half-lidded, there was nothing lazy about their look. It was intense in a way that threatened to melt my thighs. The threat increased when he said in a deep, rough-edged voice, ''I don't need designer clothes or cars or condos. I never have. That's not where I come from.'' Even deeper. ''It's not where I want to be.''

I was having trouble catching my breath. A hard swallow didn't help much. *It's not where I want to be.* My voice was thready, still I couldn't keep from asking, ''Where do you want to be?''

His gaze smoldered. ''Right here, on this floor, naked, with you.''

A bubble of air tripped down my wind pipes the wrong way. I gasped, then coughed and once again pressed a hand to my heart. In so doing, I realized that I still held the phone. Returning it to the kitchen was as good an excuse as any for leaving the hall, which had suddenly shrunk to suffocating proportions. I started to move—only to find that the cord went behind Peter's back.

Keeping myself as far from him as I could while maintaining a measure of dignity, I tugged at the cord. ''Excuse me. I'd better hang this up. If someone should be trying to call—''

I didn't finish what I was saying, because Peter had hooked his elbow around my neck, grasped the spot where my ponytail was anchored to the crown of my head and gently pulled. With the tipping back of my head, I had no choice but to look at him.

"You're frightened."

"Of course, I'm frightened. A strange man walks into my house, which happens to sit high on an isolated bluff that would do most gothic novels proud, and informs me that right then he'd like to be on the floor, naked with me. What woman wouldn't be frightened?"

"A woman who is honest about her sexuality."

"No, a woman who is nuts. Where have you been? The days of sexual promiscuity are gone. Women don't just sprawl on the floor and make love with men they don't know."

He was moving my ponytail in a light, caressive, undulating way. "You know me."

"I do not," I argued. Rays of warmth were spreading over my scalp. I fought their seduction with a spurt of anger. "Up until two hours ago, I'd never laid eyes on you."

"But you know me," he insisted in that same deep, confident, exquisitely male tone of voice. "You know that I don't jump into things with my eyes closed. I know what I want and I know how to get it. I'd never force you to do something you didn't want to do. I'd never hurt you. I wouldn't make you pregnant, unless that was what we wanted." He paused for a single, chiding moment. "And I don't have AIDS."

He'd covered everything, yet he hadn't allayed my fears one bit. He was right; I knew that he wouldn't force me, or hurt me, or give me something I didn't want to have. Instinct told me he was more responsible than most. But I didn't want to become involved with him. I didn't want to become involved with any man. After all Adam had done for me, I owed him my loyalty.

For the first time, that loyalty was being threatened. *That* was what frightened me, and the more frightened I became, the more my insides trembled as I looked up into Peter's handsome face. And the more I trembled, the more I wanted to lean into his body, to take refuge in his arms from the danger that lurked.

Which was bizarre, given that he was the danger.

Uncaring that my voice shook, I said weakly, "I have to hang up the phone. Please?"

I squeezed my eyes shut, but I could feel the heat of his gaze on my face for another minute before he finally uncoupled his fingers from my hair and stepped aside. After returning the receiver to its wall cradle, I quickly scooped up the mugs from the table and set to washing them in the sink.

Peter propped a lean hip against the counter and crossed his ankles. "Cooper said that your sister wouldn't be bothering you on the phone if it weren't for me. Is it true?"

I continued to wash the mugs, soaping and rinsing a second, then a third time.

"They're clean," he said.

I ignored him.

"Is it true?" he asked. "What does your sister have against me?"

"Nothing," I blurted out. "She thinks you're the cat's meow."

He frowned. "Have I ever met her?"

"You'd have remembered if you had." Hands dripping into the sink, I drilled him with a sharp look. "Samantha is gorgeous. So is my sister-in-law, who also thinks you're terrific. You see, their definition of terrific is wealthy and good-looking. Be grateful it's not mine. If it were, you'd be fighting me off."

"That wouldn't be so bad," he said, just about the time I realized I'd asked for it. The next thing I realized was that honesty couldn't hurt. Peter should know exactly where he stood.

"Samantha told me that I should go after you. She said that I'd be passing up a golden opportunity if I didn't seduce you, since I have you here in my clutches for the weekend. And she wasn't going to stop with the weekend. She had it all planned that I'd have you hooked by the time Monday rolled around. She thinks we need new blood in the family." I snorted. "You'd think we were vampires."

Peter didn't look particularly perturbed. "Is she a matchmaker?"

"No, she's a golddigger. She has her eye on your wallet. I'm not sure who's worse—she or Helaine."

"Helaine?"

"My sister-in-law. She has her eye on your crotch."

Peter cracked a crooked grin. "You Madigan women certainly know what you want."

"And what we don't. I don't want your wallet, and I don't want—" I darted a quick look at his fly. "All I want from you is the best possible legal defense for

Cooper Drake. Do you think you can give me that?''
I demanded in as imperious a tone as I could muster.

''I wouldn't be here if I couldn't.''

''Can you give it to me without all the other—''
the word momentarily eluded me ''—garbage?''

He shrugged. ''Sure.''

''Say it with conviction.''

''Sure,'' he said in a more forceful voice.

I wasn't sure I believed him, but the fact was that
I couldn't stand there wondering. If I was to guarantee
my safety with Peter Hathaway under my roof for the
night, I was going to have to wear him out somehow
before then.

The day was waning. I had to get to it.

3

In theory, it was a great idea. Peter wanted me to show him around, so I'd show him around—starting with an extra-long, brisk hike through the late-afternoon wind, the salt-laden air and the bracken. That would take the starch out of his pretty city shirt collar, I calculated. I felt smug in anticipation.

In practice, something went wrong. As soon as I suggested we walk into town, Peter retrieved his suitcase from the car and disappeared into the second of the two upstairs bedrooms, the spare one, the one I'd pointed him to when he'd said something about changing his shoes. When he trotted back down the stairs less than five minutes later, he'd removed the shirt I'd hoped to take the starch from. In fact, I was the one who felt unstarched. Not only had he removed the shirt, sweater, slacks and loafers that had given him a semblance of urbanity, but he'd replaced them with clothes that might well have come from Down East Army and Navy ten years before.

His sneakers had been run long and hard. Above them were a pair of basic Levi's that had been blue many washings ago but were faded now, and the fading was real. It was uneven, more so in spots that saw the most friction—the knees, the thighs and, oh Lord, the fly. Above the jeans was a faded maroon sweat-shirt, beneath the sweatshirt a gray turtleneck jersey. Hooked on a finger over his shoulder was a venerable sherpa-lined jacket.

It wouldn't have been so bad if he'd looked dirty, but he didn't. He just looked comfortable. He looked as much at ease in my kind of clothes as he did in his. I wasn't sure how it could be, given the number of hours he surely had to devote to his career to be as successful as he was, but he looked as though he spent a good part of his life in those jeans. They fit him like a well-worn glove, conforming snugly to his rangy frame, yet allowing for the movement that was uniquely his.

The worst of it was that dressed this way, he was more devastating than ever. While he still didn't look as rough as Cooper, the jeans and sweatshirt brought him close. They broadcast the fact of a hard male body beneath, and that fact did nothing at all to still my racing pulse.

I should have guessed he'd be the athletic type. A man didn't wear running shoes, a sweatshirt and jeans simply to be a paper pusher. And sure enough, when I set a hardy pace away from the house, winding over the bluffs, then across and through the scrubby pines on the long way to town, he didn't say a word. After a while, my own breathing came a little faster—frustration, I told myself—but his was as even as ever.

That was when I knew I needed Swansy. I'd intended to stop in anyway to introduce her to Peter, though I'd originally planned to do it on the way home. Swansy was a calming force for me, and I knew I was going to need something before being shut in with Peter Hathaway for the night.

I needed calming now, though. I needed to see a familiar face, hear a familiar voice, share the problem of Peter Hathaway with someone who would understand and care. Swansy was just the one.

She lived in a small, wood-frame house near the end of Main Street, which was not only the town's main street, but it's only one. I'd led Peter on the roundabout route, so we approached from the opposite direction and had to walk through town. On the one hand, that worked out just fine; I talked as we walked and was able to give him a feel for the layout of the town. The down side was that the self-consciousness I'd felt after Adam had died was nothing compared to the way I felt walking along with Peter.

Klieg lights couldn't have been worse.

But this was my town, these were my people, and I'd come a long, long way in six years. So I told myself, as I held my chin high and walked along. We passed a dozen simple frame houses on the south end of town, passed the grocery store, the hardware store, the post office and Sam's Saloon, passed the lane that led to the docks, then a few shops and a dozen more houses on the north end of town.

When we reached Swansy's, I led Peter up the gravel drive to the side door and pushed it open. ''Hi, Swansy,'' I called in a voice loud enough to carry through the bottom floor of the house. The scent that greeted me was wonderful, the atmosphere in the small kitchen warm and homey. Though I'd been well dressed for the trek from my house and hadn't been physically chilled, being with Peter was unbalancing. Already, stepping into Swansy's house, knowing that the safe and familiar was just down the hall, I felt better.

Tossing my jacket to a chair, I lifted the cover off a pot on the stove and stirred the stew inside. By the time I'd replaced the cover, a cool nose was nudging my hip.

"Hi, sweetheart," I crooned to the gentle German shepherd who'd come to greet me. Scratching her ears, I bent over to offer my cheek for a lick. "Her name's Rebecca," I told Peter as I straightened. Peter went down on his haunches to greet the dog at eye level. He looked so serious about it that I nearly laughed. Not wanting to offend him that way, I went on into the parlor.

Swansy was there, looking like a septuagenarian doll ensconced in the bentwood rocker I'd given her one Mother's Day. Little more than five feet tall, she was as slim as she was small. Though she was wrinkled enough to attest to her age, her skin maintained a softness that I'd always attributed to her complexion. Peaches and cream it was, with spots of high color on her cheeks that were as natural as the pure white hair on her head. Her smile was every bit as natural as that, and always ready.

But she wasn't smiling now. She was scowling in the direction of the television, which was tuned loud and clear to the last of the Friday afternoon soap operas. I had no sooner approached her chair when she started in.

"They do it to me every time," she complained in her sweet, birdlike warble. "Leave me hangin' right up in the air for the weekend. This time it's Babette bein' drunk and walkin' out in front of that car. We hear the squeal of brakes, and then they switch the scene. Well, I don't *want* to know that Mark is gettin' fired from his job, 'cause he'll have another one come Monday, and he doesn't even need one, 'cause he's rich as a shiek. I want to know about Babette. She's goin' to be hurt bad, and—" her warble lowered to a conspiratorial whisper "—y'know who was drivin' that car? Gordon was drivin' it. I'm tellin' you, there's goin' to be trouble, and now I have to wait until Monday to find out how much."

I smiled. "That's okay. The wondering will keep you busy." I leaned low to brush her cheek with a kiss, at the same time pressing the remote control in her lap to turn off the set. "The stew looks divine. It *smells* divine. Bettina's been up?" Bettina Gregorian lived on the outskirts of town, south to my north. She had five children under the age of nine and was not only a supermom but a supercook. She was also a superfriend. At least one morning a week, she showed up at Swansy's with the makings for something that would cook without tending and last for days. While we all looked after Swansy in this way and others, Bettina's stew took first prize.

"Stopped up first thing," Swansy confirmed. A tiny frown drew on her wrinkles. "The littlest boys have chicken pox."

"Daniel and Port? Oh, dear."

"Three weeks to the day after Mim and Sally.

She's hopin' the baby stays well. It's no fun gettin' that at six months.''

"For baby or for mother. I'll stop by tomorrow and see how they're doing.''

"Have you had 'em?''

I smiled. "When I was two, I'm told, though I don't remember, myself. I caught it from Samantha, who caught it from Ian. The maid caught it somewhere in between, and the nanny didn't know how to cook, so my mother was fit to be tied.''

"Didn't your daddy help out?''

I felt my smile turn crooked. "His way of helping was to hire a temporary girl, who proceeded to scorch his best shirts. To this day, my family talks of that time as a dark one.''

Swansy knew enough about me and my family to understand the mockery in my voice. She raised a hand to my cheek, moved it lightly, open-palmed. The gesture was as comforting to me as it was informative to Swansy. "It's gettin' colder. Winter'll be on us soon. You've been walkin' over the hill?''

She could smell it, I knew. There was a special scent, a combination of salt air and pine mist that clung to my hair and my coat. It was a dead giveaway every time.

"And your lawyer is here.'' Her hand returned to mine and held it tightly. "Please,'' she whispered. "Introduce me to him.''

A quick glance over my shoulder told me that, indeed, Peter had joined us. Ironic that Swansy should know before me, blind as she was. But her hearing was incredible. She must have heard his step.

I continued to hold her hand as I stood by the side of her chair and watched Peter as he studied her. He knew. He'd seen it right off. Whether it was Rebecca's docility that had alerted him, or the harness lying close by the rocker, or the opaqueness of Swansy's blue eyes, I didn't know, but he took it in stride.

"Swansy, this is Peter Hathaway. Peter, Swansy Tabb."

Coming forward Peter put his hand in the one Swansy offered. "How do you do?" he said with gentle formality.

"I'm doin' just fine," Swansy answered brightly. Freeing her other hand from mine, she closed it over his. "It's a pleasure to meet you."

"The pleasure is mine." He left his hand where it was, even when Swansy's top hand began to move. I wondered whether he knew how much she could tell from a hand. Either he didn't, or he had nothing to hide.

I watched her closely, anxious to know her reaction to Peter. But she wasn't letting on. Leisurely she finished exploring the back of his hand and tracking the length of his fingers. Then she wagged his hand toward a chair. "Sit by me, please."

Peter sent me a lopsided grin. In return I shot a pointed look at the cushioned armchair that sat not far from the bentwood. As Swansy released his fingers, he backed into it. I stayed close by her chair.

"Is this your first trip north?" she asked.

"No, ma'am. I've been many a time to Camden, though not in a long, long time."

"Camden." She was silent for a minute. "What was your business in Camden?"

I knew what he'd say. Camden was a summer playground for the big bucks crowd. My family and I had visited friends there many a time. Funny, we'd never heard about him then.

"When I was in my teens," he said, "I waited tables at the big old hotel that used to be there."

Which was why we'd never heard about him then. The Madigans and their friends didn't mix with the hired help. If either Samantha or I had dared to flirt with an attractive young waiter, Dad would have cut off our allowances for a month. We'd never have risked that.

Besides, the years would have been wrong. Peter was forty. When he'd been in his teens, I'd have been too young to flirt. Not that I ever really got the knack of it.

So Peter had worked. I remembered Samantha saying something—what was it?—about his having made it big only in the past five years? That opened up dozens of questions, none of which I had the nerve to ask.

Swansy did. She started with, "Where are you from?"

"Originally? Columbus, Ohio."

She mulled that over. "It's a long way from Ohio to Maine."

"Uh-huh."

Swansy pulled a Swansy, then. I'd seen her do it to others, and heaven only knew how many times she'd done it to me, but I was surprised that it worked on Peter. He seemed too sharp, shrewd enough to hold the cards to his chest in the face of a bluff. But when Swansy sat there, training her opaque blue eyes his way and smiling with such sweet anticipation, he fell prey and, without another word from her, began to talk.

"I'd been a troublesome kid. My mother died when I was ten, my older brother had long since left, and I was stuck with my dad, who was as rigid a man as you'd ever want to meet. I ran away whenever I could. Those summers, I hitched my way to the coast. I was fourteen the first time, but I was a big kid. I had no trouble finding a job. In the summers after that, my dad was pleased to see me go."

He tossed me a glance. Only then did I realize that I'd been holding my breath. I let it out slowly, but I couldn't take my eyes from him. "What did your dad do for a living?" I asked softly.

"He worked in a factory. Punched in every morning, punched out every night. I couldn't bear the thought of growing up to do that. Prison was preferable in my mind—at least, that was what I told myself when I did some of the things I did. I came really close to finding out."

"What did you do?"

He shrugged. "Petty stuff. Nothing felonious."

"Like what?"

He looked bemused. "You really want to know."

It was halfway between a question and a statement, and either way, I couldn't deny it. I wanted to know, not because it had anything to do with what he could or could not do for Cooper, but because I was curious.

"I stole cars."

I didn't say anything for a minute. Then I couldn't help myself. "That's petty? Do you know what havoc you wreak when you steal someone's car? I had a car stolen when I was twenty. It was my mother's, but I'd been the one driving, so I felt the burden. There was the hassle of being without it, the hassle of waiting for the police to call and report it found, the hassle of having it repaired, not to mention the expense, and then the feeling of driving a car that's been diddled with by some faceless creep."

Peter looked amused. "'Diddled with'?"

I'd used the phrase in all innocence, but the way Peter said it, and the look in his eye when he did, suggested something X-rated. "You know what I mean," I muttered and looked away.

Quietly Peter said, "I never damaged any of the cars I stole. I just rode them around. It was an ego trip. I stepped on the gas, really stepped on it, and watched the speedometer needle pass sixty, seventy, eighty, ninety...." His breath caught, then broke free. "It was a wild feeling of power."

My gaze had returned to his as he'd been talking, lured by the excitement that, even then, crept into his voice. It was in his eyes, too, that excitement, and as I looked it seemed at the same time dangerous and sexy. Unable to accept either, I snorted. "It was a miracle you didn't crash."

"I did," he said, and the excitement was gone. "Two weeks after my eighteenth birthday, I got drunk, went for a spin and rammed headlong into a bridge abutment. I was driving my dad's old shebang that time, so I didn't get into trouble with the law. My dad gave me up for dead, literally and figuratively. I was in a coma for a month and woke up to find that I'd broken most every bone in my body.''

I exhaled. ''What happened then?''

''Not much. At least, not quickly. I was in the hospital for months. There was a first round of operations, then a second round. I had surgery to correct things that hadn't healed properly, then I had to lie there and let them reheal. When that was done, I started in on the endless physical therapy it took to get my body working again.''

My gaze dropped to his legs. Lovingly encased in denim, they were long, strong and straight. ''It's hard to believe.''

''I could show you scars,'' he said in a very soft voice, one that conjured up tummy-tingling images.

''I'm sure,'' I said quickly. ''Still, it's hard to believe.''

''Why so?''

''You move so well. So fluidly. You don't have any sign of a limp. You kept up with me all the way from my house.'' I felt a stab of guilt. ''It wasn't the easiest walk. I'd never have suggested it if I'd known what you'd been through.''

''What I've been through is over and done. I'm fine. I swim regularly. I play tennis twice a week. I ran a marathon last month. I'm probably in better shape than I'd have been if I'd never crashed that car.'' He paused before adding, ''I know I am mentally.''

That got me wondering some more. "How did you do it?"

"Do what?"

"Get from that hospital bed to the courtrooms of America."

"It wasn't easy."

I could have guessed that, but I wanted to know the details. I raised both brows in as tempting a silent invitation as I could muster, pulling a Swansy of my own. Then it struck me that, for all intents and purposes, I'd forgotten Swansy was there.

I quickly looked to her face. She was sitting quietly in the rocker, wearing an innocent smile, as unobtrusive—and intent—as a fly on the wall. I had the distinct impression that she was pleased with the way the conversation was going.

I leaned low and murmured, "Can I get you anything?"

She shook her head, but reached for my hand. Still the focus of her attention was Peter. "How?" she asked him.

Before he spoke, he looked at me, pointed silently to the chair on which he sat, asking me with his hands whether I wanted to sit. It was a courtly gesture, but I shook my head. I felt safer standing by Swansy's shoulder, holding her hand. She grounded me.

Peter stretched out his legs and loosely folded his hands over the buckle of his belt. "I had lots of time to think when I was laid up—lots of time with nothing to do and no one to see. I felt pretty low. At some point I decided that there had to be more to life than the kind of cheap thrills I'd been looking for. So I buckled down. I took correspondence courses during my recovery and graduated from high school. I was still in intensive physical therapy, so I couldn't do much for another year. I read a lot, thought a lot. Little by little I was able to go to work. I had stacks of hospital bills to pay, and when I'd done that, I worked for another two years to stash money away for college. By the time I entered the state university, I was twenty-four. I did well, transferred to Penn, went from there to NYU Law, and the rest is history.''

He summed the struggle up so quickly that it took me a minute to ingest it. When I did, I couldn't help but let out a breath. ''That's a wonderful story.'' It was just the kind that had always appealed to me. ''You fought the odds and came through on top. There must be any number of people who are sitting back, shell-shocked to think that the drunken kid who went head-on into that bridge abutment is as successful as you are.''

''I didn't have much choice. It was curl up and die or do something with my life.''

''You could have done less. You could have gotten yourself back on your feet only enough to hold down the barest excuse for a job. You could have been satisfied with punching in and out like your father did, then going to the corner bar and drinking your way through Monday night football.''

''If that's the kind of life that works for a man, there's nothing wrong with it,'' he said in a voice that wasn't quite as gentle.

"It's a waste," I argued. "That kind of existence goes nowhere."

"For some people, it's all that's possible."

I was shaking my head even before he'd finished. "There's always more. Small things. Subtle things. There's always something to work for."

"Try telling that to the guy who can't get a better job because he can't read, and he can't read because he dropped out of school to work so his family could eat. I had friends like that. They're still back in the same neighborhood, living in the same houses, only those houses are now older and more rundown."

There were people right here in town who fit his description. "So they keep them clean. That's something. And they work so their children don't have to drop out of school to earn money to eat. So their children move ahead in ways they can't. That's something. Upward mobility is relative. You took it by leaps and bounds, and you're right, some people can't do that, but neither do they have to give up and stagnate. There's always room for *some* movement."

The movement I felt just then was the subtle squeeze of Swansy's hand. Peter looked ready to argue more, but Swansy was right. It was time to move on.

"Is your dad still alive?" I asked.

He shook his head.

"Have you kept in touch with your brother?"

Again, he shook his head.

All of which seemed very sad to me. Peter had made it, but there was no member of his family to see and share the pleasure.

Then it struck me that I wasn't much different. I had family, and plenty of it, yet I chose to keep them at arm's length. Not that they could appreciate my success. In their minds, I was a dabbler. I worked with clay for the artsy image it portrayed and sold a piece here or there. Not even the shows in New York had alerted them to the fact that I'd come into my own. But then, I told them as little as possible about myself and my success. Was I still afraid of their criticism?

Again, Swansy squeezed my hand. "It's all right," she said softly as she tipped her face up toward mine. "Some things are special, whether they're shared or not." Then she turned to Peter. "Do you think you can help our Cooper?"

"I think so. I'll know more after the weekend, after I've had a chance to look around and talk with people."

"Cooper is special."

"So I gather." He spared me a dry look, then glanced at Rebecca, who'd risen from where she'd been lying between his chair and the rocker and was nuzzling his hand.

"Would you take her out?" Swansy asked. "She likes you. She's always been a sucker for tall, good-looking men."

How she'd known Peter was tall was no mystery; she formed impressions based on how far a person's voice was above her head, or with a sitting figure, how far from the chair a pair of shoes shifted on the floor. In Peter's case, there'd also been the size of his hand and the length of his fingers. There was only one way, though, that she could have known he was good-looking, and that was from me.

That was one of the things I felt self-conscious about. The other was that Rebecca didn't need an escort. Swansy knew it, I knew it, and Peter had to know it, too. That was the only thing that could account for the cross between suspicion and amusement in his look.

I focused on Rebecca so that I wouldn't have to suffer that look.

"Does she have a favorite spot?" he asked as he stood.

"She'll lead you to it," Swansy answered sweetly. As soon as Peter and Rebecca had left the room, she tugged at my hand. I settled on the edge of the chair Peter had just left.

"What do you think?" I asked softly.

She answered as softly. "He'll understand Cooper. With a history like his, he'll be better 'n some. I think you did well."

"I can't take the credit. He was Mom's idea."

"And you're still regretting it. You're tense, girl. I'd have to be deaf and dumb not to see it. What worries you?"

"I don't know. I...don't know."

"Do you question his skill?"

"It's not that."

"Then it's something personal. He's younger than you thought he'd be."

"Yes."

"And more attractive. Are you drawn to him?"

"I'm not drawn to any man. You know that, Swansy."

"You haven't been. That doesn't mean you can't be."

"I can't be."

"Hogwash. You're a woman. You have womanly instincts."

"I can't be attracted to another man." Swansy stared at me quietly, sweetly. Inevitably, I began to talk. "I loved Adam. He was everything to me. We were like two peas in a pod, two halfs of a whole. We had something special. We shared a dream. We were going to build a life for ourselves that was pure and simple, and we were going to do it well. Just because he's gone doesn't mean I have to give up the dream."

"No one's askin' you to."

"But if there was another man—"

"It wouldn't make any difference. You'd still have your dream."

"But not with Adam."

"You're not gonna have it with Adam anyway, girl. Adam's dead."

I felt the sting of her words and wasn't sure whether I was more upset by the words themselves or the way she'd said them. I could have sworn I heard impatience in her voice. I'd never heard that from Swansy before.

Sensing my distress in the silence, she reached out and slid a withered hand to my knee. "It's the truth, Jillie. You know it as well as I do. You just won't accept it."

"I accept it," I argued. "I've *had* to accept it. I'm the one who's missed him for six years. I'm the one who's made dinner for one and then spent my evenings with no one to share the news of the day. I'm the one who's gone to bed alone and woken up alone. Adam's dead. Gone. More than anyone, I know that."

"But you haven't moved on. Think of what you were saying not so long ago to your Peter—"

"He's not my Peter."

"Well, he's more yours than mine, since you were the one who brought him up here, and don't try to distract me from the point I'm wantin' to make, which is that you've got to do something more with your life."

"More? More! Swansy, I've built an entire career since Adam died. Up to then, I hadn't done much more than sell the occasional piece in a gallery somewhere. I'm having showings in New York now, and my things are selling as soon as they're seen. Doesn't that count for doing something with my life?"

"Yes, ma'am," Swansy said with feeling. "It sure does. But what about the woman in you? You're a woman of feeling. There was more than a little of the romantic in you when you and Adam moved up here, and don't tell me there wasn't."

"I won't."

"So where's it gone? What've you done with it?"

"I've put it into my work."

Swansy acknowledged that with a pause, then a nod, then a softly warbled, "Yes, you have. It's one of the things that makes your work special and different and beautiful. You put your feelings into that clay.'' Her voice grew even softer. "But what about the rest, Jillie? What about the rest of the dream?''

I swallowed. I knew just what she was thinking. She and I had discussed it often in the months before and after Adam died. We hadn't discussed it in a long, long time.

Looking down at my hands, I said, "It's not that important. I've been lucky with my career. It's more than I could have asked for. It'd be selfish of me to think that I can have everything. No one has everything.''

"You wanted children.''

"I can live without them.''

"Why should you have to?''

"Because Adam's dead. I wanted Adam's children.''

"And if you'd fallen in love with another man before Adam, you'd have wanted that man's children. You are a nurturer. I see it here. You nurture every one of us in your own special way, but it's not the same as having children of your own.''

"I have all of you, and I have my career. I'm perfectly satisfied with that.''

"Are you?''

"Yes!''

"Then what is it about your lawyer that makes you nervous? If you're perfectly satisfied with your life, how can be pose a threat?''

"It's no big *thing*. The man makes me nervous, that's all.''

"Because you're attracted to him, just the way you should be, and you're feelin' guilty, 'cause you're still married to Adam, only Adam's dead, so's you have every right to be attracted to Peter, only you're shaky like a young girl, and you don't like that.''

"Damn right, I don't.'' Mostly I didn't like being analyzed so well. Blind as she was, Swansy saw right through me, and I didn't like what she saw. "First Samantha, now you. What is it with you people? Do I tell you how to live your lives?''

"Yes, you do. You told me that I should have a dog. You said that if I had one, I'd be more independent. Think of it, independent, at my age. But you were right. I listened to you, and you were right.''

"Listen to me, hah. I had to make all the arrangements behind your back, then tell you that Rebecca had nowhere to go but here because she was allergic to smog.''

"And it worked. So what about you? Should I tell you that Peter Hathaway has an ulcer and needs a cure by the seaside?''

"An ulcer?'' came a deep voice from the door. "That's an interesting thought. Actually, I'd forego the ulcer and just take the cure by the seaside. It's great out there, all woolly and wild.''

Attesting to that was his thoroughly tossed hair, his ruddy cheeks and his eyes, which held added life as they homed in on me. The collar of his jacket stood up against the back of his neck. He looked healthier than a man of forty had a right to look. And more virile.

I couldn't think of a thing to say.

But Peter wasn't done. He said to Swansy, ''Why would you want to tell Jill that I had an ulcer?''

In the flash of an instant, I imagined what Swansy's answer would be. I decided to beat her at her game. "So I'd take pity on you and take you in," I said in a brassy tone. I rose from my chair and started toward him. "She thinks there's something missing in my life. Not only should I take you in, she thinks, but she thinks that I should let you father my children." I made a small sound of disgust. "Can you believe that? She hasn't known you for more than twenty minutes and she's got you and me having kids."

I slipped past him, raising my voice as I returned to the kitchen. "You're being a *busybody*, Swansy, and it's not right. I know what I want and what I need, and I don't need a husband any more than I need children. My life is full." I grabbed my coat from the chair. "Very full." I shoved my arms into the sleeves. "If I wanted kids, there are a dozen guys up here who would volunteer their services," I started back toward the parlor, "and if I wanted a husband, I'd find my own. But I don't want either. I'm doing fine. Just fine."

Stalking past Peter, I went to Swansy's rocker, put a hand on either arm and leaned low to kiss her cheek. "I do love you, though," I whispered. "You'll be okay?"

Swansy touched my cheek and nodded.

"Should I put dinner on the table?"

"I can do that myself," she warbled, but didactically. "I can do it because I've accepted my weaknesses and moved on. I'm learning to do things I didn't think I'd be able to do. I've grown."

Her message couldn't have been more blunt if

she'd framed it in neon and stuck it in front of my nose. But I couldn't get angry; I'd used up my allotment for the day. And this was Swansy. I loved her like—sometimes more than—my mother. She was there when I needed her, comforting me when I was blue, laughing with me when I was high.

So she'd spoken out of turn this time. She'd earned the right.

"I'll stop by tomorrow," I said, then straightened and passed Peter again on my way to the back door. I had no desire to wait while he said goodbye to Swansy. I didn't want to hear any words that might be exchanged between them. I'd about had it with being the brunt of other people's good intentions. I was very definitely on the offensive.

Dusk was approaching when I led Peter back down Main Street, then down the lane that led to the dock. "The *Free Reign*," I said, gesturing toward the sturdy trawler that bobbed by the rotting wood pier. She was secured both bow and stern by heavy ropes that I could only think of as manacles, and the way she tugged at them, while maintaining her pride and presence, reminded me of Cooper.

His house was next on our list of stops. It was conveniently situated at a midway point on the lane. Though smaller than the frame houses that corded Main Street, it was clearly well tended, in fine repair. I wanted Peter to see that.

With a single rap of the brass knocker, I opened the front door, which put me right into the small living room. Cooper was there, straddling a bench before the fire, creating a work of art with a piece of wood and a small knife. He was surrounded by shavings. I guessed that he'd been furiously working off his frustration since he'd left my house, but the boat he was carving didn't seem to be suffering any from the frustration. It was still in its early stages, still nearly as much a log as a model boat, but there was a gracefulness to the part he'd carved that promised good things ahead.

I wanted Peter to see that, too.

Quietly I crossed to the fire. "Are you okay?"

Cooper's dark eyes slid past me to Peter, then returned to mine. With a brief nod, he returned to his work.

"I was worried."

"No need." He chipped off a sliver of wood, chipped off a second, chipped off a third.

"I'm trying to give Peter a feel for the town. We've been to Swansy's. I thought we'd stop off at Sam's for dinner. Will you join us?" I wanted that more than anything. Having dinner alone with Peter came second only to spending the night alone in my house with him on a list of things I was dreading.

But Cooper wasn't cooperating. "Not tonight, Jill. I'm not much in the mood."

"Maybe it would help cheer you up," I suggested, but even as I said it, I knew it wouldn't. Cooper's look made that clear. His sharing a table with the big-time lawyer from New York would be broadcasting his dilemma to the world. It didn't matter that this world already knew his dilemma; the broadcasting would dig at him much as he dug at his log, chip after chip after chip.

"Is Benjie around?" I asked. Not only did I like the idea of his being with Cooper, but I wanted to introduce him to Peter.

But Cooper said, "He's not back yet."

I frowned. "Wasn't he due back yesterday?"

"He called to say he was staying till tomorrow."

Benjie Drake and New York City weren't the best twosome in the world. Benjie had always been a little on the wild side, and though Cooper rode him hard, there was only so much he could do. It wasn't as though Benjie was a kid anymore. He was an adult. He earned a living working on the boat. Or used to.

"There's not much for him to do here," Cooper said in echo of my thoughts. "I don't much like his being there, but if I raise a stink, he may just decide to stay." He chipped off one sliver of wood, then another. "I can be patient."

"Do you do much of this?" Peter asked. He was standing before the stone mantel with his hands in his pockets, pinning his jacket open. His eyes were on the boat that sat there. It was a finished model—or as finished as Cooper ever made them. Upward from midpoint in the hull, it was an intricately carved schooner; downward from that point, it was rough-hewn, blending into the log from which it had been carved and which now served as its stand.

"It's a hobby," Cooper said in a flat tone.

Taking one of his hands from his pockets, Peter touched the boat with much the same care that he'd touched my pieces earlier that day. "I wish I could do this," he said quietly and with utter sincerity. "I don't have any artistic ability at all. My handwriting's so bad that in my office, decoding is a major secretarial prerequisite."

I watched the way his thumb smoothed wistfully over the wood. "Your strength is with words," I said. "And legal strategies."

"Maybe, but I've always admired people who could make things like this. Art is way up there, on a plane by itself. It's a beautiful outlet for a whole world of emotions."

"Swansy and I were just saying that," I said on impulse and regretted it seconds later when Peter looked suddenly curious. "You said it much better than we did, though. You do have a way with words." I turned quickly to Cooper, who had paused in his whittling to witness my exchange with Peter. "You'll be coming over tomorrow afternoon?"

Cooper hesitated for several seconds, during which his eyes once again told me that he didn't want to be working with Peter. I held mine steady. No way was I yielding. Peter Hathaway was going to clear Cooper of the charges against him, and that was that.

"I'll be there," Cooper said, and there was a tiny movement at the corner of his mouth that, magnified, would have denoted wryness. "If I'm not, I'll never hear the end of it."

"You're right."

"You're tough."

Cooper was the one person beside Swansy who knew how untough I really was. "Oh, yeah." I turned to Peter. "All set?" I wasn't sure whether he had any questions for Cooper or whether he was satisfied to wait until the next day to really get started.

His touch lingered on Cooper's boat for a final minute before he returned his hand to his pocket and cocked his head toward the door. With a wave to Cooper, I led Peter on.

We stopped next at the grocery store, where I picked up additional food for the weekend—additional, because though I'd already stocked up on the basics, I knew they weren't going to be enough. Part of it had to do with the way Peter had downed two thick tuna sandwiches without blinking. The other part had to do with his size. He was lean but solid. His shoulders alone, I figured, would warrant extra bacon and eggs and milk.

When I turned toward Sam's Saloon after leaving the grocery store, Peter paused. "Shouldn't we have saved the shopping for last," he peered into the bag he held, "so nothing spoils?"

"It would have been too late. Claude's closing."

"But it'll be another hour or two until we get back to your place."

"No problem. Sam has a huge refrigerator. He'll put the bag there while we eat." He did it all the time for me. It was, I supposed, one of the perks of living in a close-knit community. I couldn't imagine any of the pricey restaurants that my family frequented in Phillie offering such a service. But it was a nice touch, like Claude's keeping my charges on account, payable at my convenience, or Greta's special-ordering me the latest paperback bestsellers from her distributor, who stopped by the drugstore monthly to refill the single small rack with books.

Everyone knew everyone else here, which meant that when I entered Sam's Saloon with Peter, we created something of a stir. It was a small one; the people who lived here were private, even shy, certainly laconic in the way that was typically Maine. But we had their attention, almost to a man.

With Peter in tow, I headed for the kitchen. I responded personally to those who called out as I passed—a smile for Tom Kaskins, a wave to Joan Tunney, a wink at Stu Schultz. These people were my friends. I enjoyed seeing them. By virtue of their presence, I didn't feel quite so alone with Peter.

Sam Thorn, owner and chef of the Saloon, was in the kitchen. One look at me and he burst into a grin wide enough to rival his girth. "I knew there was a special reason I made lasagna tonight," he teased.

I adored his lasagna. Though I'd had lasagna in little Italys around the world, Irish-born Sam's was the best. Of course, he had the edge on ambiance. The Saloon was a thoroughly relaxing place to be.

And I did relax. After stowing my groceries in Sam's fridge, I settled across from Peter in a booth and let Sam treat us not only to his lasagna, but to Caesar salad and garlic bread. Sam, himself, kept us company for a bit, then others stopped by to say hello.

They were curious about Peter, I knew. They were also timid, unsure of what to say to him. As mild as he was, as smiling and patient, they were awkward. It didn't matter that he looked very much like them in his dress, in the wind-muss of his hair and the late-

day shadow on his cheeks. In their eyes, he represented glitz, and glitz was foreign to them.

It wasn't foreign to me, still I knew what they felt.
In his own subtle way, Peter was larger than life. He'd
seen more, done more than we had, and he ran in
circles that I'd given up on fitting into long ago. Had
he and I been alone, I'd definitely have felt awkward—though how much of that would have been
due to his looks alone, I wasn't about to wager. For-
tunately we weren't alone for long.

Steven Willow, whose family had run the hardware
store for three generations, stopped by to quietly ask
what I thought about his buying a computer. "To
keep watch on inventory," he told me. "Paulie says
we should."

"Paul is a student at the Community College," I
told Peter. "He's taking business courses." To Steve,
I said, "It's worth looking into. Computers cost less
now than they used to. Would you want to use one?"
I knew that the major force against modernization in
a town like this was habit. Steve's answer supported
that.

"Not me. But Paulie. He'll be takin' over one
day."

I thought about that for a minute before repeating,
"Look into it with Paulie. There are probably uses
you'd have for a computer besides the one you'd be
buying it for. It might be well worth the money."

With a two-fingered salute of thanks, he moved on,
only to be replaced several moments later by Noreen
McNard. She was one of the town's newest residents,

having married Buck McNard, Jr., only two years before.

"My parents are coming to visit," she told me after shyly greeting Peter.

Noreen came from northern Vermont. Since the drive was a long one, with precious few superhighways on the way, she didn't see her parents often. She'd been particularly lonely of late. I was pleased for her now. "That's exciting! When?"

"Next Friday." Her eyes sparkled. "A week from today. They'll stay the weekend." She was slightly breathless. "We'll give them our room. We can sleep in the attic." Her eyes widened, her voice lowered. "But I don't know what to cook."

"No problem. I have dozens of good recipes."

"I'm a terrible cook."

I squeezed her arm. "You are not. I tasted your potato salad at the fair last month, and it was great."

"But that was *her* recipe," Noreen whispered. "I can't serve her everything she taught me to make. She has those things all the time. But I ruin every new recipe I try."

"You won't ruin mine. You can't. I have nine years' worth of fool-proof recipes. None of them has more than five ingredients. It's impossible to spoil them." I saw glimmers of hope and relief in Noreen's eyes. "Want to come by on Monday and we'll go through my file?"

"That would be great," she said with a grateful smile. Still smiling, she lowered her eyes and darted a self-conscious look at Peter. "Pleasure meeting you," she murmured and scurried off.

Peter watched her leave, then arched a brow my way. "You're a regular consultant. Is it always this way when you hit town?"

I shook my head. As though to contradict me, Noel Bunker chose that moment to walk up. I dragged in a breath, feeling vaguely sheepish. "How's it going, Noel?"

"Okay."

I introduced him to Peter as the owner of the local gas station and a good friend of Cooper's. Peter took that in, as he had all the other information I'd given him on people we'd seen or talked with, but he didn't ask questions. I assumed he'd taken to heart my warning about the townspeople being wary, but in any case, it was a wise move on his part. He was giving us time to get used to having him around, which implied that he was going to be around for a while.

I didn't like the idea of having him around for long.

I didn't want to *think* about having him around for long.

So I looked up at Noel and asked, "How's Lisa?"

"'Bout the same," Noel answered. Kneading the pocket of his checkered wool jacket, he added, "We got to do something."

In a quiet voice, I explained to Peter, "Lisa is Noel's daughter. She's seven. She broke her leg this summer. The cast has been off for four weeks now, but she's still not walking right. The doctors say that the pain will go away, but the leg just doesn't look right."

"Has it been X-rayed?" Peter asked.

"Oh yes. They say the broken bones have knit, but

I wonder how well." Feeling Noel's worry as my own, I looked up at him. "Can I get the name of that specialist?" I'd been offering to do it for two weeks, but Noel and his wife had resisted. Until now.

Noel nodded. He continued to knead his pocket, as though the wool were worry beads.

"First thing tomorrow," I assured him gently. "Boston's a little closer. Should we try there?"

"Guess so."

I knew he was feeling low and tried to convey encouragment in a smile. "Done. I'll get a good man, Noel. Lisa will be fine."

He nodded at me, nodded at Peter, then moved on.

"They love you," Peter said, picking up where he'd left off before Noel had arrived.

"It's mutual. These people are real people. They may not say much, but when they do speak, you can bet it's the truth, and I love them for that."

"But they *love* you. You're their guru."

That embarrassed me. "I am not. I've just had more experience than they have in the world beyond this town, so they come to me with their questions. I like being involved in their lives. They sense that, I suppose, and that encourages them to come back. If I weren't here, they'd find the answers all by themselves—" I paused "—but I don't usually tell myself that. These people make me feel needed. Illusion or not, I don't care. I like the feeling."

Indeed, I did. I was in my element here. Among these simple and unpretentious people, I felt as fulfilled as I ever did—except when I was home, in my attic studio, pouring my heart and soul into slabs of clay. They were two different kinds of fulfillment. The first gave me satisfaction as a human being, the second as an artist. But there was a third kind of fulfillment, one that I became acutely aware of several hours later as I prepared for bed.

Wearing my long white nightgown with lace at the hem, wrists and high collar, I sat on the end of my bed and listened to the sounds of Peter preparing for the night in the room beside mine. My cheeks grew pink, my palms damp. Against my wishes, my body tingled in places where tingling wasn't allowed.

I wondered then about the kind of fulfillment that a woman can only get in the arms of a man, and I prayed that the urges I felt were passing ones. Because I wasn't about to experience that kind of fulfillment again—particularly not with Peter, who was the kind of man Adam might have been, had I not led him off to the sea.

4

"Wake me at nine."

They were the last words Peter said to me before closing the door to his room, and they echoed in my brain for most of the night. When I finally fell asleep—after trying in vain to read, then trying in vain to do a crossword puzzle, even creeping upstairs and trying in vain to sketch out the glaze pattern for the fruit bowl I'd thrown earlier that week—it was nearly one in the morning. I awoke again at two-thirty, four fifty-five and six-ten, and each time the same thing happened. I turned over and came slowly to consciousness, then opened my eyes with a start when I remembered that Peter was there. With that recollection came a simultaneous jumping in my stomach that was a long time in settling. When I finally gave up the fight at seven-fifteen and climbed out of bed, I wasn't at my best.

Wake me at nine.

The hands of the small stove clock crept. It wasn't that I was eager for Peter to be up and with me, because I certainly wasn't. I had nothing to say to him. He was here for one reason and one reason alone— to defend Cooper. I assumed that he planned to spend the morning in town chatting with whomever he could find who'd be willing to open up on the subject. That was fine with me. If he thought he'd just sit around the kitchen, dawdling over breakfast for several hours, or hang around the living room—or worse, my studio—that wasn't so fine. I wasn't sure I could take it. He might just as well sleep later.

It appeared that that was just what he was going to end up doing. At nine on the dot, I went upstairs and knocked on his door. When there was no answer, I knocked again. After a minute, I accompanied a third knock with his name, but even that failed to elicit a response. So, slowly and cautiously, I turned the knob and eased the door open.

Peter was sprawled facedown on the too-small bed. One bare arm was hooked over its edge and hung nearly to the floor, the other was curved under the pillow. The covers cut diagonally across his body, starting beneath his right arm and ending at his left hip, and beneath the covers, his legs were widespread. I even detected his feet conforming to the vertical end of the mattress.

My stomach was at it again, jumping in the way that had become familiar during the night.

I looked toward the ceiling, but that didn't do much good. In the minute that I'd studied what was on the bed, certain things had etched themselves indelibly on my mind. Such as the hard muscles of Peter's shoulder. The dark tuft of hair beneath his arm. The firm flesh at that spot on his hip that would normally be covered by briefs.

Helplessly my gaze fell back to the bed. "Peter?" I called softly, then wondered why I wasted the effort.

If my knocks hadn't woken him, a soft call wouldn't. Something stronger was needed.

"Peter!" I called more sharply, then, in annoyance as much as anything else, "*Peter.*"

He stirred. He moved his legs, then his hips, but when he went still again, it was clear that he'd simply made himself more comfortable.

"*Peter*!" I shouted. I was beginning to feel mildly panicked. If he didn't wake to my voice, I was going to have to shake him, which meant putting my hand on his skin. I wasn't sure I could do that.

"Hmmm."

I breathed a sigh of relief. It hadn't been much of a sound, but it had been something. "It's nine o'clock, Peter. You said to wake you at nine."

He turned his head on the pillow so that I could see his face. His eyes were still closed. "Mmmm."

"It's nine." When he didn't respond to that, I said, "Peter?"

"I hear," he grumbled groggily and turned his head the other way.

I had the distinct impression that he was going right back to sleep. "Are you getting up?"

"Ten," he mumbled. "Wake me at ten." The words were slurred.

Eager for any excuse to leave the room, I said, "Fine," and backed out, closing the door behind me.

That left me with the dilemma of what to do with my time. What I'd planned to do, before Peter had popped his little surprise about wanting me for his girl Friday, was to work. But an hour wasn't much time. No sooner would I have everything set up than it would be ten, and at ten I was supposed to wake him again, and that meant breakfast soon after, and Lord knew when he'd be finished. By that time whatever I'd been working on would have dried out.

So I ruled out working. I'd already showered, dressed, made my bed, dusted my room, as well as dusted and dry-mopped the entire downstairs, which was really quite funny, since I'd done it all just the day before. But there was something to be said for expending nervous energy, and I was filled with that.

Baking seemed like a good idea.

I wasn't normally any more compulsive a baker than I was a cleaner. Though my family occasionally mentioned my having gone north to commune with the sea and bake my own bread, I'd never gotten into that routine. Oh, I'd tried. It was truly a romantic thought, and there was nothing more divine than the smell of fresh-baked bread. But I never seemed to do it quite right. My bread came out looking deformed, and all too often the smell that filled the kitchen was of something burning. Far easier, I decided, to buy my bread at the store.

Muffins, on the other hand, were my pals. Mix everything in a bowl, pour into paper-lined muffin tins, bake. Very easy.

Over the years, I'd made the standard blueberry muffins, corn muffins and bran muffins. With the taste of success, I'd grown bolder. Among my repertoire were apple-nut, zucchini and wheat germ, cottage cheese and chive, even ones heavily laced with dried fruit and rum.

Today I decided on cranberry-pumpkin. I had a bag

of fresh cranberries in the fridge and several cans of pumpkin on the shelf. The other ingredients were all staples. So I went to work.

Two dozen muffins were in the oven baking when ten o'clock rolled around.

Wiping my hands on the dishtowel, I went upstairs. I tried knocking first. After all, Peter was a new acquaintance. I couldn't just barge into his room, assuming familiarity simply because he'd been in a dead sleep earlier.

I discovered to my chagrin, after repeating the ritual of knocking, then calling his name, then timidly opening the door, that he was still in a dead sleep, sprawled much as he'd been at nine.

"Peter?" I waited, then raised my voice. "Peter." I waited, then shouted, "Peter!"

He shifted. "Hmmm."

"It's ten. You said to wake you at ten."

He neither moved, nor made a sound.

"Peter."

Nothing.

I couldn't help but wonder whether he always slept this soundly, or whether he was doing it to annoy me. If the latter was so, it worked. Taking the few steps necessary to reach his bedside, I shook his shoulder. "Peter! It's ten!"

I snatched my hand back. Annoyed or not, I was affected by the firmness of his shoulder and the warmth of his skin.

He shifted, inhaled a deep breath, stretched.

I thought I'd die when the covers slipped to reveal twin dimples at the top of his buttocks.

I bit down hard on my lower lip to give myself something to think about, but the pain I caused wasn't half as interesting as those dimples, or the virile plane stretching above them, or the finer, paler skin under his arm, or the sprinkling of freckles across his shoulders.

Move, I told myself, but I couldn't budge. I'd never seen anything that had as debilitating an effect on my knees as the body spread before me.

"Ten o'clock," I sang out in a high, shaky voice. "Get up, Peter. It's ten o'clock."

He turned his head on the pillow, opened an eye and did his best to focus, without much success. I was ready to put money on the fact that he didn't know who in the devil I was—and I felt more than a little peeved, even hurt by that—when he said my name. It wasn't much more than a tired moan, but it was my name.

"Jill."

"Got it in one," I said in that same, higher-than-normal voice.

He barely moved his lips. "What time is it?"

"Ten."

Moaning, he turned his head away. "I should have been up at nine."

"I woke you then, but you told me to come back at ten."

"I'm so tired."

I hadn't considered that. I'd been too preoccupied with my nervous energy to think about why Peter was having such trouble waking up, and it wasn't as though the nervous energy was gone. But it had changed. As I stood there, unable to move from his bedside, it had become something softer and sweeter, something that I wanted to call exciting.

"What were you going to do this morning?" I asked. I was feeling the beginnings of compassion for the man. He seemed so zonked.

"Walk around," he mumbled. "Check out the local police."

"What time is Cooper due here?"

"One." He stretched again, this time half turning to his side, and in the instant before he drew his top leg up, I caught a glimpse of a line of soft, dark hair on his belly. My heart reacted wildly, and my eyes shot upward, following that line as it widened in a spray of hair over his chest. I had just focused on a small, brown nipple when it disappeared beneath the covers, which Peter drew up.

A helpless little sound slipped from my throat. Horrified, I coughed to cover it up. Between that cough and the newly risen covers, the spell was broken.

"Are you getting up?" I asked as I headed back toward the door. I didn't care that I sounded cross. Enough was enough.

Apparently not. "Eleven. Wake me at eleven."

"Oh, Peter."

"I'm beat. Too many late nights."

That's your problem, bud, I was on the verge of saying when he added, "Had to clear my desk to get here."

I should have known he'd say something like that, something I couldn't berate. I sighed. "Eleven?"

"Mmmm."

This time when I closed the door, I made no attempt to cushion its click. I didn't slam it, just... closed it. And I trotted down the stairs the way I normally did, washed the mixing bowl without taking care to be particularly quiet, talked full voice on the phone to an old friend in Boston about an orthopedic specialist, even turned the radio on to the country sound that I liked. When I'd done everything I could in the kitchen, I trotted up to my studio and did some organizing of materials, which entailed the opening and closing of cabinets. Then I trotted back down to take the muffins from the oven. While I was at it, I put on a pot of beef stew to cook. My recipe was nowhere near as good as Bettina Gregorian's, hers having far more ingredients than I could cope with. But while there wasn't the subtlety to my stew that there was to hers, it was still remarkably good.

At eleven o'clock, I put on my most nonchalant front and made my way back up the stairs. I didn't bother to knock this time, or call Peter's name from the door. For expediency's sake, I went straight to the side of the bed, took a firm grasp of his upper arm and gave it a good, solid shake.

He jumped. His head shot around, eyes opening wide on mine, though they didn't seem to see a thing. After several taut seconds, he slowly closed his eyes and sank down to the bed, but on his back. He threw an arm over his eyes. "You scared the hell out of me," he said in a quiet voice.

"I'm sorry. There didn't seem to be any other way to wake you."

"Is it nine?"

I had to smile. "No. Eleven."

He lifted his arm and peered up at me. "Eleven. I was supposed to get up at nine."

"When I woke you at nine, you told me to wake you at ten."

"Then ten."

"When I woke you at ten, you told me to wake you at eleven."

That gave him a moment's pause. "I did?"

I nodded.

"Oh." He dropped his arm back to his eyes. "I was having the most incredible dream."

Adam used to say the same thing. Then he'd reach for me and expect that I'd be as aroused as he was, only it didn't always work that way. If I was sleeping, I was sleepy, and if I was awake, my mind was on other things. Adam thought about sex a lot. I didn't. In my book, there were far more important and exciting things in our relationship than that.

Without conscious intent, my gaze slipped over the covers toward Peter's groin. But he had a knee bent. I couldn't see a thing—for which I thanked my lucky stars the instant I realized what I'd gone looking for. If he'd been hard, I wasn't sure what I'd have done.

Then again, if he hadn't been hard, I'd have wondered more.

Then *again*, maybe my mind had gone suddenly wicked. Maybe his dream hadn't been sexy at all. Maybe he'd been dreaming about winning one case or another.

I wasn't about to ask. Instead, I cleared my throat. "Are you awake now?"

"I think so."

"Help yourself to the shower," I said as I took my fill of his chest. It was solid, impressively broad at the shoulders, tapering to the waist where the covers lay, and it was a devilishly masculine blend of bone, muscle and flesh. I saw the tracings of several faint scars, but like the small one high on his cheek, they only added to the allure. "There's plenty of hot water. I had a new heater put in year before last."

"Sounds good."

"Bath towels are in the cabinet under the sink." I wasn't sure if I'd told him that the night before, but, if so, the repetition didn't hurt. I tried to think of what else he'd need to know, but I was distracted by his ribs. They weren't harshly delineated—he wasn't that lean—but they provided an interesting contour to go with the swell of his pectorals and the faint concavity of his stomach.

"I made muffins," I said quickly. "I'll put eggs and bacon on when you're ready to come down-stairs—unless you'd rather not have eggs. I can understand that you might not, I mean, if you're keeping tabs on your cholesterol level. Lots of men are, now-adays. And women. I can skip the eggs. It'd be no trouble. I have cottage cheese and yogurt and plenty of fruit—"

It was as if I ran out of breath, just like that. One minute I was talking, the next minute I wasn't. Every-thing seemed caught up in my throat, because while I'd been babbling, Peter had slid his arm back on his forehead. Thus uncovered, his pale green eyes were focusing on me, holding my gaze captive, seeming to control the rest of me, as well. I couldn't move. Nor could I think of anything but the intimate message being conveyed, not only by those eyes but by his pose. With his arm up high like that, the entire upper half of his body was lifted, extended, made to look larger and more imposing than ever.

I sucked in a sharp breath when his hand—the one that had been lying innocuously on the quilt—closed around my wrist. He tugged. I resisted.

"Sit," he commanded quietly. His eyes continued to hold mine.

I shook my head. "Not a good idea."

"Why not?"

I couldn't think straight—at least, that was what I told myself when I didn't offer an answer. I wasn't about to say that his body excited mine too much for me to sit. I wasn't about to say that I was frightened not of him, but of myself.

He tugged harder, and I found myself perched on the side of the bed smack by his hip. Wisely, from his point of view, he didn't release my wrist; if he had, I'd surely have bolted, because my pulse was already running a frantic race and threatened to drag the rest of me with it. Rather, he anchored my cuffed hand to his chest. I curled my fingers into a fist, which was the least I could do to protect myself from the lure of his flesh.

"I shouldn't be here," I whispered.

"Why not?"

"I have things to do downstairs."

"Like?"

I tried to think, but it was difficult, being so close

to him. All my energy seemed sidetracked in the effort to keep my breathing steady. I swallowed. "Like...see to the stew."

"Stew takes care of itself."

I knew that, but I'd hoped he wouldn't. "Do you cook?"

"I used to. It was a matter of survival."

The story he'd told at Swansy's about his crude beginnings came back to me in a rush. It was hard to remember he'd been mortal once. "You must eat out a lot."

"Enough. Sometimes it's just grabbing take-out on the run. I'd do more cooking if I had the time. I like cooking."

I couldn't believe the conversation. Peter had just bolted out of a dead-deep sleep, it was eleven in the morning, he was lying in bed half naked—all naked, if the truth were told—smelling faintly but deliciously of sleep-warmed man, and we were talking about cooking?

I wished he'd lower his arm. There was something exquisitely intimate about a man's armpit. Maybe it was that not many people saw it. Maybe it was simply that it was different; I shaved mine. The hair under his was soft and smooth, as was that sweet skin beneath it.

Funny, but I'd never paid particular heed to Adam's armpits. Or maybe I had, but I'd forgotten. Six years was a long time. A long time.

"Are you disappointed in me?" came the deep voice that was not Adam's but Peter's.

My eyes flew to his. "For what?"

He shrugged with one shoulder. "I don't know." But his eyes told me otherwise. In their probing green way, they said that I'd been looking entranced with his body one minute, then not so entranced the next. "Oversleeping, maybe," he improvised when I said nothing. "You hired me to work, not to sleep the weekend away."

How could I be angry when he'd obviously needed the sleep? "You were tired." I tried to casually lift my hand away from his chest, but he wasn't letting go.

"Leave it there. It feels good on my skin."

"It shouldn't be there. I shouldn't be here. You're right. I hired you to work, and now I'm distracting you."

"You're the boss. You can do what you want."

But I couldn't. I seemed to have lost control of my senses. That was the only explanation I had for not jerking my hand free and fleeing the room. Peter wasn't holding me *that* hard.

But I stayed. I stayed because I was in the thrall of the soft, sweet, exciting feelings that were surging through my insides. They were new and pleasant. I wasn't ready to oust them just yet.

"Why were you so tired?" I asked. "Were you really up late all week clearing things up so you could come here, or did you just say that to make me feel guilty?"

He frowned. "Did I say that?"

"Yes. When I tried to wake you at ten. Is it true?"

"Yes and no. There was a lot of stuff that needed to be taken care of so I'd be free, but I also had a crisis situation with one of my clients.'' My raised brows invited him to elaborate. He took them up on it. ''I defended the man on charges of embezzlement. He was convicted on lesser counts than he'd originally been charged with, but he was still sentenced to a brief prison term. Last Monday there was a brawl in the prison yard. He's been accused of stabbing one of the other inmates.''

''Oh dear.''

''Oh dear is right. He would have been out on parole in another two months. Now he's facing disciplinary action that could add another six to his sentence.''

''Is he guilty of the stabbing?''

''He did it, but he claims it was self-defense.''

''Were there any witnesses?''

''Yeah. A prison yard full, all of whom hate my man because he isn't one of them. He's really a straight guy who made a single big mistake in life. Now that's been compounded. And the worst of it is that he has a wife and two kids. The pressure was so bad in their neighborhood that they moved, but they've been waiting for his parole to start putting the pieces together again.''

''What could you do for him? Were you able to help?''

''I was up there every night this week trying to keep him cool. At the same time I was talking with every official I could get my hands on, trying to stop what's happening. We're talking white-collar crime, here. My client doesn't know from physical violence. But if this thing escalates, he's gonna learn real quick, and that's gonna make it twice as hard for him to fit back into the mainstream of life when he gets out. I mean, if we're talking justice, let's have justice.''

I could feel his tension beneath my palm.

My gaze fell. Sure enough, my fist had relaxed into a hand that was open on his chest, shaping itself to the gentle swell of muscle there. I stared at it, stared at the comparative slimness of my fingers and the way soft wisps of dark hair fringed their tips. I didn't dare move—not my hand or my arm or my body or anything that might dislodge my fingers from the heavenly groove they'd found.

''Jill?''

My gaze flew to his face.

''What are you thinking?'' he asked in a voice that was deeper and more throaty than it had been moments before.

Thinking of that tone of voice, knowing the meaning of deeper and more throaty, I snatched back my hand—successfully this time—and said in a rush of words, ''I shouldn't be with you here. It isn't right. You've come to defend Cooper. That's all I hired you for. It's all I want.''

He lowered his arm. ''Is it?''

I gave a convulsive nod. ''I don't care what Samantha or Helaine or Swansy or anyone else says, I'm not available.''

''You're a widow. You're not married. You say there isn't anything going on between Cooper and you—''

''There isn't.''

"Then with another man? One of those stunning men you say are up here?"

It looked as if I wasn't going to live down that overheard conversation. For a minute, I wondered if I wanted to. I should lie, I mused. I should tell Peter that there was another man. He'd never know the difference.

But he would. He'd make it his business to know, and, given that he was going to be in touch with most of the townspeople over the next days and weeks, he had the means at his fingertips.

Closing my eyes, I let out a breath. "No, there is no other man." I opened my eyes and looked into his. "But I have no intention of getting involved with anyone in the kind of way you're thinking. I had a wonderful marriage. I feel a deep loyalty to my husband. He left me a house, a boat, a way of life and a wealth of memories. They're more than enough for me."

"Are they?"

"Yes."

"Is that why your body reacts to mine the way it does?"

I swallowed. "I don't know what you're talking about."

"Sure, you do. Every time we look at each other something hot and sexy passes between us."

"No," I said and shook my head, only to become aware that Peter's hand was curled around my neck. His thumb traced the outer shell of my ear.

"It's there, Jill, and it's mutual. We don't have to be touching, but it's there. And the closer we get, the stronger it is.'' He took my hand, the one I'd snatched back and was holding in a fist against my stomach, and returned it to his chest. Unfurling my fingers, he dragged them up until my palm lay flat on his heart.

"Feel it?" he asked.

I couldn't have missed it. It was like broken thunder. *Ka-thunk. Ka-thunk. Ka-thunk.*

"Yours is like that, too."

"No."

"Yes." Locking my eyes with his, he slid his hand from my neck down the column of my throat, over my sweater to my breast. Fingers splayed, he covered my heart.

Move, I told myself, but I couldn't budge. The whole of me seemed trapped beneath that large hand. Everything that I'd been and done and wanted for the first thirty-one years of my life seemed suddenly suspended. Only my heart moved. *Ka-thunk. Ka-thunk. Ka-thunk.*

In the gentlest of motions, he contracted his hand until it lightly kneaded my breast. I felt a corresponding contraction deep in my belly and sucked in a lungful of air, which served to offer that much more of me to his touch. My body swelled and tingled. I couldn't think of anything but how nice that felt, how deep, how rich.

Suddenly the heat left my breast, and he closed his hands around my upper arms and drew me forward and down.

"No," I whispered.

"Just a kiss," he whispered back. He continued to draw me down, now with his hands on either side of my head, but it was his eyes that drew me most strongly. I could see darker shards among the light green there, and though those shards were mossy, they smoldered.

I felt the smoldering to the tips of my toes, a heat that poured through my veins like a flash of white-hot light, sending sparks radiating outward all along the route. I'd never, never felt anything like it before, neither with Adam nor with any other man who'd chanced to look at me with desire. But I wasn't so naive that I didn't know what it was. I was in the midst of a passion attack so intense it scared me to death.

"No, please—"

His mouth touched mine. The sensation was so light, so new, so pleasurable that I gasped. He took advantage of that small parting of lips to deepen the kiss. But he wasn't a marauder. As though he knew how frightened I was, he caressed my mouth with slow, gentle, moist strokes. He nibbled here and sucked there. And he kept on doing it, kept on doing it until all I could think about was how lovely it felt. I didn't have to give; I simply received. Even when he broke the contact to try a different angle, he was the one to turn my head to the angle he sought.

I was stunned, because the pleasure increased with each second that passed, and with each one of those seconds, the fear seemed to fall away, well into the periphery of that kiss. I was caught up in it, caught up in the texture and heat and scent of it.

I'd never been a particularly sexual being, had never given much thought to the individual aspects of lovemaking. A kiss was a kiss, pleasurable, yes, but still only a kiss. I'd never dreamed that a kiss could make my mind whirl, but that was just what it was doing, which was why, when he whispered, "Open your mouth for me," I did.

That was the extent of the demand he made. Once more he was the doer, the taker. He explored the insides of my lips, drew the lower one into his mouth and sucked on it, sought out and stroked my tongue in a way that offered such delight that I opened for more.

It seemed to go on forever, which was just what I wanted. I wasn't in a rush to go anywhere. I had nothing to do that was more pressing than exploring the outer reaches of the pleasure Peter's mouth offered. So I gave myself up to his ministrations without a peep.

At length, and reluctantly if the last, lingering touches were any indication, he separated our mouths. I had had my eyes closed, but when I realized that my lips were alone, I opened my eyes. Though his were heavy-lidded, he was watching me closely.

"Don't," he warned just as I was about to stiffen. "Don't make something wrong about what was very right, and *don't*—" he caught me opening my mouth "—say it wasn't right, because it was. I've been around a lot, and I know the difference between right and wrong. I'm not saying that there has to be anything more. We may have just hit the apex of our relationship. Maybe that's as good as it gets with us. But it was good. Don't tarnish it by getting your back up. It was just a kiss. Just a kiss. There is no grand commitment in a kiss.''

I wasn't so sure. Something had definitely changed in the course of that kiss. A barrier was down. I no longer felt quite so strange sitting on the edge of the bed with Peter in it. I felt as though I had a right to be there.

Which was rationalization enough not to move, though I did pull my hands back from his chest and tuck them in my lap.

Peter settled back on the pillow. He left one hand on my arm, as though ready to catch me if I decided to flee. It was the mildest of restraints, but welcome. If I wouldn't be able to escape, I reasoned, there was no point in trying.

"Tell me about you, Jill. Tell me what makes you tick.''

I stared at him for a minute, then tossed a wide-eyed look at the ceiling. ''That's an impossible order,'' particularly when I was still feeling warm and light-headed from his kiss. ''I wouldn't know where to begin.'' I was looking for direction from one who was more experienced in coping with the post-passion-attack muzzies.

Peter was just the one. ''Why are you here? I know you said that you came here to pot, but we both know you could have done that back home. What made you leave?''

''I grew up. I got married.'' When he waited expectantly, I added, ''I couldn't very well set up house with my husband in my childhood bedroom.''

''I'll bet it was a beautiful bedroom in a beautiful

house,'' Peter teased so gently that I couldn't take offense.

"Yes to both."

"Big brick thing? Ivy on the walls? Lush grounds?"

"You've seen it."

"No. But I know the area. I've represented people from that neighborhood."

I thought of the Humphreys. They weren't the kinds of family acquaintances I was proud of. It was one thing for Peter to represent them, that was his job, but it was something else for my father to pal around with a man who'd done what William Humphrey had. My mother kept a discreet distance, still I was amazed that the friendship hadn't hurt her career.

"Then you know just what it's like," I said.

"I know that I'd have given my right arm to grow up in something like it. So it's hard for me to understand why you left."

"It shouldn't be so hard. There are some distinct similarities between being born at the top and being born at the bottom."

"Oh yeah?" he drawled. "I'm listening."

"You're slotted. Whether at the top or the bottom, there are certain expectations you're supposed to meet. At the bottom, you're supposed to be rough, down-trodden, angry. At the top, you're supposed to be self-assured, socially adept and glamorous. In either case, there's a mold to fit into. I didn't fit into mine."

He moved his hand on my arm in a light, gently soothing motion. "I can't believe that."

"It's true."

"But you're all those things you mentioned."

"I'm none of those things—or I didn't used to be. I've come to be pretty self-assured in the past few years, and I guess I can pass in the socially adept department when I have to. But glamorous? I've never been that." I hurried on, lest he think I was fishing for compliments. "Oh, I'm pretty enough. But glamorous is more than just looks. Glamorous is an aura. It's high gloss and sophistication. It's knowing the right people and frequenting the right places. It's seeing and being seen. That all makes me very uncomfortable."

Just thinking about it, I felt shadows of the old nervousness that used to haunt me day after day. My hands involuntarily tightened in my lap. "My parents are comfortable with that kind of public life. So are Ian and Samantha. I guess I was cut from a different mold. That life never fit me quite right, and it wasn't as if I didn't try. I tried for nearly twenty years. I figured that if I tried long enough and hard enough, at some point things had to click, but they never did." I looked him in the eye. "So to answer your question, I left because I'd had it with trying to play the part of a Madigan. I was tired. I wanted to be myself."

Peter's hand lay still on my arm. He seemed totally engrossed in what I was saying. "Maybe you're right," he conceded. "Maybe there is a mold. But you have to fight, really fight to break out of the one at the bottom. From the top you just...drop out."

I had to make him understand that it wasn't as simple as that. "It's still a fight, Peter. In my case, there were endless confrontations in the library at home. Yelling and screaming may seem petty compared to what you went through, but to me it was a nightmare. I've always been a pacifist. That's one of the reasons I never fit in well at home. They're always fighting. Always. And about *really* petty things.'' I shuddered. ''Believe me, I had to fight to break free.''

At my shudder, Peter's hand began moving again. ''Do you see them often?''

''Once or twice a year.''

''In Phillie?''

I nodded. ''They won't come here. It's just as well. Given the opportunity, they'd pick my life to pieces. So I go down there.''

''On holidays.''

''Not if I can help it. Holidays are happier up here. I usually just pick an odd weekend to visit.''

''They must be pleased to see you.''

''For the first five minutes.''

''Then what?''

''Then we start fighting. I have my own ideas about things. In recent years, I've been more inclined to voice them. That's what I mean, I guess, about my being more self-assured than I used to be. My life up here is like an anchor. I feel secure here.''

''Maybe that's because of the friends you've made. Maybe if you had friends like that in the other world, you'd feel more secure there.''

''I have lots of friends back home.''

''Friends from the old life. The Madigan life. Not ones you really like or trust, or you'd be back to visit more often.''

I couldn't argue with him there. He'd effectively summed up the situation. It actually surprised me that he had, since he'd started the discussion from the other side of the fence. Big city, big name, big bucks—still he was different from the people back home. Maybe it was his background. Maybe it was just him. He didn't only listen; he heard. I had to respect that.

"Don't you ever miss the city?" he asked. The hand that had been on my arm fell down to capture one of my hands. He linked his fingers with mine. I didn't fight him. His touch was pleasurable.

"No," I answered lightly, much as I had every time I'd been asked that question during the past nine years. Then I paused. I looked down at our hands. There was something so natural, so honest about the way they were linked that I found myself confessing in a small voice, "Some things. Sometimes." My eyes quickly sought his. "But they're small things. Like visiting museums. Going to favorite restaurants. I could do them if I wanted when I go back to visit, but I usually don't bother, which means that I don't miss them all that much."

"Would you have done them with Adam?"

"Sure. Adam and I always had a great time when we did things together."

"Would you do them with me?"

I took in a deep breath to say, "Sure," nearly as automatically as I'd said it before, only the sound didn't come. Certain thoughts intruded, thoughts about opening myself up to grief. After all, Peter wasn't Adam.

Very softly, I said, "You wouldn't want to be a stand-in for another man. That's not your style."

"Damned right it's not. I wouldn't be a stand-in for Adam, any more than you'd have me for one, and we both know it." His voice lowered to a dangerously seductive level. "And you won't scare me off with that line, Jill Moncrieff. I've touched you. I've kissed you. And you weren't thinking of Adam when I did."

He was only part right. Thoughts of Adam had flickered through my mind, but by way of comparison, and Peter had come out ahead each time. That bothered me.

"Would you do it?" he asked softly.

"Do what?" I asked, feeling cross.

"Spend time in the city with me? When you come in for your show, I could take you to—"

"I don't know if I'll be going in for the show. I told you that."

"You could if you wanted to. It's your decision. We could have a nice time, Jill."

I could just picture his idea of a nice time. "Oh yeah, in a suite at the Plaza?"

"Why would I want a suite at the Plaza—"

"For the seduction you obviously have in mind. You're transparent, Peter Hathaway. I have you pegged."

"I was thinking of taking in the Metropolitan Museum and the Museum of Modern Art, going to a few shows, your taking me to your favorite restaurant and my taking you to mine. And there'd be no reason at all for a suite at the Plaza, when I have a perfectly good place on Central Park South—"

"See? I'm *right*! You have *one* thing on your mind."

"I do *not*!" He held both of my hands, now tightly. "I have a two-bedroom place, just like you do here, and I meant what I said about doing those other things. I'd enjoy them."

"You probably do them all the time."

"I don't. I've been to the Metropolitan Museum six times, and each time it was for a charity benefit. I've never been there to see the art. Same for MOMA." He was the one who seemed cross now. "And if you think I'm proud to be saying that, you're nuts. But the fact is that I haven't wanted to do those things alone, but I've never found someone I wanted to do them with."

His crossness added credence to his words, as did the fact that he looked embarrassed by what he'd said.

"You don't have to sit there looking so smug," he muttered. "I don't have the cultural background you do. You were probably eight years old when they took you to a museum for the first time. I never, ever went. I've come a long way. I've taught myself lots of things over the years. I can hold my own in most any situation, but there are still some where I feel uncomfortable."

"Art museums?"

"Yes."

"And I wasn't looking smug. I'm surprised. That's all. And touched." Small snatches of vulnerability in a man so strong were very appealing. I was beginning to feel the force of that appeal building newly inside me.

Apparently Peter was beginning to feel something, too, because in the next instant, he came right up off the pillow and captured my mouth with his. I had no chance at all to protest; one minute he was lying flat on the bed looking vulnerable enough to kiss, the next he was doing it.

Not that I would have protested. I'd enjoyed his last kiss too much, and the instant his lips covered mine, I felt an explosion of the same intense pleasure. Actually the pleasure was even greater this time. I wasn't sure how that could be, but this new kiss seemed to have an army of feelers that were spreading joy through my body, finding and scratching niches I hadn't known I possessed.

Peter was right about one thing; something felt very right about this kiss, which was why I let it go on, let it go on just a little longer. It was a big mistake for two reasons. The first was that the longer he kissed me, the more hungry he grew, and the more hungry he grew, the more of himself he put into the kiss and the more excited I became. The second was that somewhere between a tongue thrust and a lip suck, a loud cough came from the door.

As one, and in alarm, Peter and I followed the direction of that sound to find Cooper's tall, dark frame filling the doorway.

5

The only comparable experience I had to being found by Cooper in a compromising position with Peter was being caught with Jason Abercrombie in the Abercrombie's Newport boat house showing him "mine" in exchange for a look at "his." We were five at the time, and I handled it well. I giggled.

I didn't know what in the hell to do now. Giggling sure wouldn't do it. Nor would jumping up and straightening an imaginary frock like a mortified maiden. I couldn't begin to think of the ramifications of Cooper's having caught us this way.

Bewildered, I looked at Peter, and in that instant several things struck me. The first was that, even sitting, he was taller than I; my eyes just reached his nose. The second was that, somewhere in the mindless course of his kiss, my hands had slipped around him; my fingers were clutching him dangerously low on his hard, bare hips. The third was that that kiss had stirred up a storm in my belly that was in no way diminished by Cooper's arrival.

Given my choice, I'd have sent Cooper away and gone back into Peter's arms.

Of course, I could think that precisely because Cooper *was* there. He was my safety net. If he hadn't appeared, I'd be terrified by the train of my thoughts. As it was, all I had to worry about was Cooper's respect for me, Cooper's respect for Peter, Cooper's willingness to work with Peter after what he'd just seen—just seen? *Continued* to see.

With slow, measured movements, I withdrew my hands from Peter's skin, but my eyes didn't leave his. Silently they told him of my inner fear and begged him to say something, do something to salvage the situation.

For a minute there, I could have sworn Peter was as bewildered as I was. It was very subtle, but I'd spent so much time looking into his eyes that I could recognize something different when I saw it. I knew that he was thinking about the very same things I was.

To my relief, he took in an uneven breath, straightened his shoulders and cleared his throat, but it was to me he spoke, and in a quiet, intimate tone that suggested a new bond between us. ''I could use some of that breakfast you mentioned before—eggs, bacon and whatever muffins smell so good. Why don't you go on downstairs? I want to talk with Cooper for a minute, then I'll shower and be down.''

His voice wasn't so low that Cooper couldn't hear what he said, and since there was no immediate objection coming from the door, I guessed that Cooper was in favor of the talk. I swallowed, took a breath of my own and slipped from the bed. Though Cooper moved aside to let me pass, I stopped when I reached him and looked up into his face. I wanted to apologize, or explain, but to do either would be an insult to Peter.

So, mustering a shred of humor, I said, "Watch what you say to him. He's got nothing on. A man can get very defensive when he's naked." Without allowing him time for a rejoinder, I left the room and went directly downstairs.

Several minutes later, I was working off my worry beating eggs when I heard the shower go on upstairs. Within a handful of seconds, Cooper entered the kitchen. Determined to be nonchalant, I said, "Will you have breakfast? I made fresh muffins."

"It's a little late for breakfast."

The stove clock read noon. "Brunch, then." I frowned. "You're early. You weren't due until one."

"I was sitting home, wondering what he was doing to earn the hefty fee you're paying him." He paused and added dryly, "Interesting what I found."

I would have felt awful had not I caught sight of the faint twitch at the corner of his mouth. "You think this is funny," I accused.

Cooper gave a tiny move of his head that I knew for a shrug. "What I think," he specified, "is that I'll never forget the look on your face when you turned around and saw me there."

I was embarrassed. "You should have called from downstairs."

"I did."

"Oh." Again I caught that twitch, and while I didn't begrudge Cooper a moment of lightness what with all else he was going through, I wished it weren't at my expense. "What did he say to you?"

"That his intentions are honorable."

I snorted. "Sounds like he thinks you're my father."

"Not exactly. He asked if I minded the competition."

"What did you say?"

"I said that I wasn't competition for him, but that if he ever did the slightest thing to hurt you, I'd tear him apart."

It was the kind of Cooper statement, offered without the slightest show of emotion, that made me love the man. Unable to resist, I threw my arms around his neck and gave him a tight hug. I stepped back before he could protest. He wasn't one for grand demonstrations of affection. I never liked to push the issue.

"I'm glad you're here," I said, then quietly went back to making breakfast.

"Are you sure you want me to stay?"

The question was loaded. I looked him in the eye. "Yes. I want you to stay."

"You wouldn't rather be alone with him?"

I'd come to my senses. The passion attack was over. I could think clearly again. "No. Stay, Cooper." I looked down at the bacon I was trying to separate. "I don't want to become involved with Peter, but it's like there's a force that pulls us together. At the height of the pull, I'm someone else. All the rest of the time, I'm me. It's…disturbing."

Cooper was silent for a minute. "Then take it slow."

"Fine for you to say. Ever tried to stop a wave

from breaking?'' I eyed him beseechfully. ''How do I do it, Cooper? How do I stop it?''

''Do you really want to?''

''Yes.''

''Why?''

''Because it's pointless. It has nowhere to go. I don't have room for a man like that in my life.''

''Come on, Jill.''

''I don't!''

''You have room. You could make room.''

He was serious. I couldn't help but be reminded of the comment he'd made the afternoon before about my buying a condo in the city with the money I was willing to spend on legal fees. ''It's time,'' he'd said, and he was serious then, too. He'd never said anything like that to me before. I wondered whether the change had something to do with the smuggling business, and, if so, what.

''If I didn't know better,'' I said, ''I'd think that you were encouraging me.''

''I think you should follow your instincts.''

''But what about Adam?''

''What about him?''

''I loved him.''

''I know you did. But he's dead. You won't be breaking any rules by enjoying Peter.''

''You *are* encouraging me.''

He repeated that small semi-shrug. ''You could do with a good tumble.''

''Cooper—''

''I'll stay for breakfast, Jill. And I'll stick around after that if you want me to. But I can't stay forever.

If it isn't Peter, it'll be another guy someday. You weren't meant to be a widow forever. You're a beautiful person. You deserve more than that.''

As I studied Cooper in the aftermath of his words, I wondered—and not for the first time—why he and I had never become more deeply involved. I supposed that Adam would always come between us, but there was more to it than that. Something was missing. The spark wasn't there. Thank heavens it was mutual, or our friendship would never have worked. I cherished that friendship.

''Just stick around,'' I whispered through a tight throat and went at the bacon again. Beside me, Cooper put a fresh pot of coffee on to brew. We worked in a companionable silence for a time until Peter joined us. Then preparation for Cooper's case began in earnest.

The rest of the weekend was dominated by that case. I wasn't sure whether Peter was compensating for having been caught fooling around, or whether he was that dedicated to the law. I didn't think it was that he'd lost interest in me, because though he didn't try to kiss me again, the awareness remained. It was there each time his eyes lit on mine, whether he was reviewing facts with Cooper in my kitchen, or talking with the townsfolk in their homes, in the back room of the grocery store or in Sam's Saloon.

Still, he didn't try to kiss me again.

Saturday night he stayed downstairs reading long after I'd gone up to bed. Sunday morning he slept late again, but when I knocked on his door at the appointed hour of eleven, he awakened quickly. Not long after that he came downstairs for breakfast newly showered and looking ruggedly handsome in his limb-loving jeans and sweatshirt. I was surprised that he hadn't brought down his bag. I had expected him to leave that day to drive back to New York, but it seemed that he planned to spend the entire first half of the week with us.

I wasn't sure whether I was pleased or not.

"It makes sense to do all the groundwork now," he explained. "The more I know at this point, the more effectively I can decide what has to be done to put together a good case."

The problem was that we weren't coming up with anything new. Granted, the townspeople were nearly as close-mouthed as I'd feared, still they talked. We spent time with nearly two dozen different people, and neither Peter's gentle questioning nor my supporting presence succeeded in prying out information that would be a help to Cooper. We learned that he was well liked and respected, which I, for one, already knew. But no one could prove a plausible motive for diamond smuggling—for either Cooper or any of his crew. With the exception of Benjie, we spoke with each member of that crew, and though they were nearly as wary as their neighbors, we couldn't find anything in what they told us to merit a second look.

By the end of Monday, we'd scoured most of the town. Sitting down with Cooper and me over dinner that night, Peter talked frankly about his plans.

"Barring a major attempt on our part to pin the blame on someone else, our best hope does lie with establishing reasonable doubt. We have plenty of character witnesses, including your police chief. I'll go over my notes and decide which of the people I've met will be the strongest witnesses. I'm driving down to Portland tomorrow morning to meet with Hummel. Since he's the U.S. Attorney who'll prosecute the case, he has certain information I want—at least, he should have it. His is the burden of proof. One of the things he'll try to suggest—'' Peter eyed Cooper ''—is that you've been involved in things like this before. That means he'll be back-checking your bank records to try to find evidence of past large, unexplained deposits.''

''There are none,'' Cooper said. He swiveled Peter's ever-present pad his way, took up a pencil and wrote down the names of the three banks at which he had accounts, plus the rough profit he made each week. ''Deposits are always in this amount. Interest speaks for itself.''

Peter nodded. ''Okay. When Hummel sees this, he'll go looking farther. He'll put an investigator on the computer looking for other accounts. Are there any?''

''No.''

''What about investments—stocks, bonds, real estate deals. Anything I should know about?''

''No.''

''No plane reservations for a trip to South America?''

Cooper's look told him what he thought of that idea.

''So,'' Peter concluded, ''his case will consist

solely of the discovery of those diamonds in your cabin in a laundry bag with your name stenciled on it. We've definitely got a set-up here.''

"By whom?'' I asked. I'd wondered about that a lot. "Who would have put the diamonds there? Is there a ring of gem thieves that the authorities have been watching? Who were the diamonds originally stolen from? And who tipped off the Customs people to check out Cooper's boat?''

Peter gave me one of those looks that was at the same time professional yet oddly intimate. "Those are just a few of the questions I intend to put to Hummel tomorrow.''

So Tuesday morning he drove to Portland. I offered to go with him, but when he told me it wasn't necessary, I didn't push. Clearly he felt there were some things he could do better without me, which was just fine by me. I was actually relieved. I needed a break from those devil eyes of his. And I needed to work.

I spent the day at it, and a productive one it was. The tall vase that I threw had a particularly interesting twist to its lines; the pieces I glazed and fired were similarly inspired. Moreover there was a normalcy to working in my attic studio. It was reassuringly familiar and right in ways that Peter wasn't. I was pleased to be alone with my work and my thoughts.

Not that my heart didn't do it's little catch thing when the time approached for Peter's return, or that the little catch thing didn't magnify into a wallop when I heard him come in. But that was all physical, I told myself, and physical I could overcome.

It helped that we spent the evening with Cooper,

though I doubt Cooper saw things that way. He was having a difficult time with Benjie, who had returned from New York and didn't want any part of Peter, or me, or Cooper, for that matter. He said hello, then goodbye and headed for the back door. He wanted to be in Bangor visiting with his latest girl.

Cooper had other ideas for him. ''It can wait,'' he said finally. ''I want you to have dinner with us.''

Peter and I were in the living room, Cooper and Benjie in the kitchen. The house was small enough so that we could hear every word.

''Come on, Coop,'' Benjie complained. His voice was that of a man, though his whine was nowhere near. ''She's waited six days. If I ask her to wait any more, she's goin' to bolt.''

''You should've thought of that when you stayed longer in New York. I want you here, Benj. You can do what you want tomorrow, but I want you here tonight.''

''I don't have anythin' to say to that guy.''

''Then you can sit and listen to us talk.''

''Give me two hours. Two hours, and I'll be back.''

''You're staying here.''

''One hour.''

''You can see her tomorrow.''

''You can't do this to me, Cooper. I'm old enough—''

''Damned right, you're old enough, and that means you have certain responsibilities...''

His voice grew more distant, until we could no longer hear the words. I assumed he and Benjie had moved into the back hall, and I felt immeasurably relieved.

"Nothing like being forced into eavesdropping," I whispered to Peter, who looked as though he knew what I meant.

"Do they always fight?"

"Usually. I don't understand Benjie. Cooper's been so good to him over the years without asking a thing in return. You'd think Benjie would *want* to do something. You'd think he'd be concerned about what's going on. But he couldn't care less."

Peter's voice stayed as low as mine. "Maybe he doesn't know what's at stake."

"He knows. He was here with us right after the arraignment. He knows Cooper could end up in jail."

"Does he think Cooper's guilty?"

"He says Cooper was framed, but the way he says it is incredible. Pure fact. He knows the answer—a frame—that's all there is to it. And when he's done saying that, it's like he has nothing more to say. The discussion's over. He washes his hands of the whole thing." I gave a low grunt. "Much as I love Cooper, Benjie isn't one of my favorite people."

"I get the impression you're not alone," Peter said. "To a man, the people we've spoken with have had good things to say about Cooper, but what about Benjie? No one ever grouped them together. No one ever volunteered information about Benjie. When you stop to think of it, they were very happy to skip over him as though he didn't exist."

"That was generous of them," I decided. "Benjie's been in and out of trouble for years. More than one of those people have been at the butt of his pranks. Forget pranks—he's been known to shoplift. Can you believe that? In a town this size, where everyone knows everyone else, he shoplifts.''

''Maybe that's why he does it, because he knows his victims. He knows they like Cooper. He counts on Cooper getting him off the hook.''

''Which is exactly what Cooper does. The two of them disagree on most everything, but Cooper's nearly always the one to give in.''

''I'm surprised they work together.''

''Cooper insists on it.''

''I'd think Benjie would object.''

''Are you kidding? He may be just this side of juvenile delinquency, but he's not dumb. He knows a good thing when he sees it.''

''Does he work?''

''In his fashion. I'd say he's with the boat on maybe seven out of ten trips, and even then I doubt he works as hard as the rest of the crew. What other job could he have where he's paid well and can do most anything without risk of being fired?''

''Cooper has his hands full.''

''I'll say. Benjie is gorgeous, and he knows it. He can also be a charmer when he sets his mind to it. It's a dangerous combination.'' As always when I thought about Benjie, my heart went out to Cooper. I was angry on his behalf, angry at Benjie.

Being able to sound off like this was a luxury. ''He has a mean side, Benjie does.'' I sent Peter a reproachful look. ''He's the type to feed firecrackers to a duck. He's the type to take joy in eating bacon from a pet pig. If he were a little older, a little smarter, a little more traveled, I'd be looking closely at *his* bank account. He'd be just the type to stash diamonds in his brother's cabin and then keep his mouth shut when the trouble started. In any case, you can bet he's not sorry the *Free Reign* is impounded. That means Cooper can't make him work.''

''If he doesn't work, he doesn't make money. So how does he support trips to New York and cute little numbers from Bangor—or shouldn't I ask?''

''You shouldn't ask.''

Peter looked mildly dismayed. ''Cooper seems like such a down-to-earth, straight-thinking sort. Doesn't he know that he's not doing the kid any favors by covering for him that way?''

''I'm not sure whether he does or doesn't. You have to understand Cooper. When he feels strongly about something—one way or another—he feels *strongly* about it. He doesn't do things in half measures. His loyalty to me is a prime example. So's his indulgence of Benjie. The kid is his little brother. He adores him. He can be firm, but only to a point. When push comes to shove, he gives in.''

''It didn't sound like Cooper was giving in just now.''

''Just wait. He'll be back without Benjie.''

Sure enough, several minutes later, Cooper returned alone. ''He's gone to Bangor,'' he said tightly. He ran a hand through his hair, and for a minute I thought he was going to say more on the subject of Benjie. But he simply dropped his hand, turned toward the door and said, ''Let's go.''

We drove several towns over to a restaurant that was owned and run by friends of mine, a pair of displaced Baltimorians who offered the closest thing to nouvelle cuisine to be found in these parts. Cooper hated the menu, I could tell. He was a meat-and-potatoes man, and though I was usually partial to similar simplicity, I found the variety of offerings welcome.

So did Peter, which surprised me. I would have guessed he had nouvelle cuisine coming out of his ears, but he claimed that the regional specialties made this menu different. We had fun running through the choices, had fun teasing Cooper when he couldn't make up his mind.

The food was wonderful, as I'd known it would be, which was why I'd chosen this particular restaurant. I wanted to impress Peter. I wanted him to know that we Mainers had our own pockets of sophistication—though Cooper, bless him, seemed bent on denying it. He had dry comments about the table setting, the food when it finally arrived, even the other diners, and though I doubt he intended it that way, he was really quite funny.

I felt surprisingly good, and the two glasses of wine I'd had—a Puligny-Montrachet that Peter ordered—had little to do with it. I was pleased to be out with these two men—Peter, who excited me, and Cooper, who made the excitement safe.

For the first time in months I'd dressed up, which wasn't saying much by city standards, but it was a switch for me. It was also something that the Friday before I wouldn't have thought I'd enjoy doing, but enjoy it I did. On a whim, I'd worn a wool suit that I'd bought in Phillie the year before. Though it wasn't much more than a slim, knee-length wool skirt, a silk blouse and a hip-length blazer, more businesslike than dressy, with the double strand of pearls that my parents had quite hopefully given me when I'd turned eighteen, I felt feminine.

No doubt some of that feeling came from my legs being exposed. I didn't miss the way Peter stared at them when he first saw me, then kept stealing little looks from time to time. Nor did I miss the way he looked at my hair, which I'd washed and blown into a gentle pageboy that pooled on my shoulders. He'd never seen it down like that. Either he had a thing for long hair or for blond hair, because he seemed intrigued. And that made me feel good.

In fact, I was feeling *so* good that it was a lucky thing Cooper came back to the house with us, or I'm not sure what I'd have done. But he came inside and sat down with Peter to ask where the case went from there.

For the next hour or so, Peter told of all he hadn't learned from Hummel, then launched into a discussion of petitions, motions and writs. I tried to follow what he was saying, but I kept getting distracted by one thing or another. First it was his mouth, lean and hard and masculine as he talked. Then it was the contrast between his crisp white shirt and his rich brown hair, then the fine hairs on the back of his wrist, just barely visible beyond the sleeves of his dark blue blazer, then the way his gray slacks flexed with his thigh as he threw one knee across the other. Then it was back to his mouth, which held me for a fancifully long stretch.

Then my eyes grew heavy, and the next thing I knew, Cooper was shaking me awake. "Better me than him," he said with a pointed glance at Peter. I had the distinct impression they'd discussed who would do the shaking, even had a laugh or two over it. Though I wasn't wild at the thought of that, I had to be pleased that, despite their differences, they were getting along. Then again, those differences weren't as great as I'd originally thought. Peter was not to the manor born, as I'd been.

Not that I cared. In fact, at that moment I didn't care about much of anything but going to bed. It had been a long time since I'd had wine, *plus* an after-dinner drink. I was feeling it.

Not so Peter. I didn't know how long he stayed in the living room talking with Cooper, but when I awoke the next morning—granted it was nine and absurdly late for me—he'd already put the coffee on to drip and was in the process of making something that smelled incredibly tempting. Using Bisquik, some apples and the confectioner's sugar he'd found on the shelf he'd created the lightest apple pancakes I'd ever tasted. He said he'd added a secret ingredient, but when I figured out that there were already five ingredients that I could count, I didn't bother to ask him what it was. I wouldn't make a recipe that had six ingredients. Better to let Peter make them for me again.

Better to let Peter make them for me again.

As soon as I thought it, then did a double take on

it, I rejected the idea as unwise. Still, after we'd spent the morning talking with the harbormaster, who was also the town manager and the resident historian, after Peter had stowed his bag in the Saab for the return trip to New York and turned to me, I couldn't resist asking, "When will we see you again?"

"Is that the royal 'we'?" he teased.

I shrugged inside my coat, feeling shy in a way I hadn't felt before.

His eyes held mine. Like a beacon in the fog, their luminescence spread through every bone in my body, making my awareness of him crystal clear.

"You are like a royal," he said, and his voice was no longer teasing, but low and a little rough. "You're different from the people here. You may not want to believe it, but you are. And they know it. I've seen it in the way they approach you. They give you the kind of deference saved for someone of special stature. It even happened at the restaurant last night. You're a princess. The Madigan heiress."

"But they don't know about my background. I don't talk about where I come from."

"That's part of the mystique." His eyes didn't leave mine as he mulled over the word. "It is a mystique. On the surface, you're what you chose to be, a woman who has given up the city in favor of the simple life of an artist on the coast. But you're more complex than that, and the things that you are, the things you were born to be, refuse to be totally buried. They come out in your manner, in your approach to problem solving, in your tastes—" He paused and said even more softly, "But that didn't answer your question, did it?"

I was a little stunned that he'd given such thought to my character. It was even more flattering than the attention he'd paid my legs the night before. "No," I murmured.

"That's because I don't know the answer. There's a lot of work to be done from my office. Most of it's legal work, technical stuff, but there's research, too. I'll call Cooper when I have questions for him. And you."

Did that mean he'd call Cooper when he had questions for me? Or call *me* when he had questions for me? Or call me sometime, questions or no? He was telling me *nothing*, which made me wonder all the more. But I didn't want to sound unduly interested, so I didn't press. And then the opportunity was gone when Peter took me by the arm and walked me back to my door.

I looked up at him. The wind was playing havoc with his hair, styling it just the way I liked it. "Will you be driving all the way through?"

"I'm not sure." He seemed distracted. "I'll play it by ear. See how I feel."

"You ought to stop for coffee, at least. It's a long way."

He said nothing to that. When we reached the front door, he guided me over the threshold, then turned to face me. I looked up at him and swallowed hard. He seemed so serious.

And so dear—that thought caused my heart-catch

this time. Contrary to what I'd expected, contrary to what one part of me wanted, I *liked* Peter Hathaway.

"Thanks for everything, Jill," he said in a low, deep, slow voice.

His sincerity embarrassed me. "I promised a hotel. It was a little unconventional, I suppose, and you had to make your own breakfast this morning, but it was shelter against the wind."

"That it was," he murmured, and in the pause that followed I could have sworn I saw a wistful look. "I'm going to miss you."

My heart caught several more times in quick succession, then sped on. Frightened to think of where that would—or wouldn't—lead, I fought it with a grand show of bravado. "You are not," I scoffed. "You're going back to the city, to your busy practice and your associates and your exciting friends and the Beautiful People who throw interesting parties several days a week. You're going back to that two-bedroom condo on Central Park South, which will probably look like heaven compared to what you've seen in this town."

"Not heaven. Just New York."

Wistful—sad—I couldn't quite figure it out and then understand it. Big name, big city, big bucks couldn't really be sorry to be leaving, could he?

"Come here," he growled. Taking me by the elbows, he drew me to him, and, in the same fluid motion, lowered his head and commandeered my mouth. His lips were like a fire out of the cool ocean air. His kiss was a scorcher.

It was what I'd wanted, what I'd feared. It set the

fires inside me burning with an intensity not to be believed. It was, I supposed, the culmination of several days of exchanged looks, remembered heat and good, old-fashioned, lusty imagination—and I had to confess that I was as guilty as he was. But that didn't excuse it by a long shot.

Was it right? It sure felt it, but that was probably what Eve had thought when she neatly cupped that apple in her hand and took a big bite. The difference between Eve and me was that I couldn't just stand there and chew, debating the pros and cons. I was weak-kneed, for one thing, and had to slide my arms around Peter's waist for support. For another thing, the hunger in his kiss was stirring my blood and making me dizzy, meaning I couldn't think straight.

It seemed to be a recurrent malady when I was around Peter, but it was at its worst when he kissed me. His mouth was wet and hot, eating at mine as though he hadn't had a meal in days, which indeed he hadn't, if the time were counted from our last kiss. He was making up for the lapse, using not only his lips, but his teeth and tongue to stoke the fires that crackled within me.

And it wasn't only his kiss that was doing me in. It was his body. The way he'd drawn me to him had brought us together in a way we hadn't been before. Our coats were open; our bodies touched, more than touched, pressed, strained. His arms were around me inside my coat. One splayed hand was exploring my upper back, the other was open on the seat of my jeans, holding me close. I could feel the hard muscles of his chest, the hard muscles of his arms, the hard muscles of his thighs. City man though he was, he was ruggedly male. That maleness made me buzz.

I'd never been as turned on by a man's body before. Through a haze of light-headedness, I was aware of the length of his legs, which gave him the height to make me feel delicate, and the breadth of his chest, which made me feel feminine. I was aware of the leanness of his waist beneath my hands, then the ropey muscles of his back when I slid them higher. I was aware of the angle of his chin and the firmness of his lips and the fact I was tipping up my head to better grasp his kiss.

Along with all of these things, I was aware of a growing need, a rising expectancy in my body that cried for assuagement. Peter was giving me a taste of heaven, but a taste was no longer enough. So I went looking for more. For the first time, I took part in the kiss. I nipped at his mouth as he'd done to mine, stroked his tongue, sucked his lips. I discovered that being an active player in the lovemaking was heady, but it didn't give me the relief I sought. When the tingling in my breasts became uncomfortable, I rubbed against him to ease the ache, and when he backed me to the doorjamb and leaned into me, I made room for his leg between mine. There was an ache there, too. He ministered to it with the insistent pressure of his thigh, while he brought his hands forward and covered my breasts.

I cried aloud at the explosion of sensation and was panting when his mouth left mine. His own breathing was rough against my cheek as he held me still for a

long, painful moment. The last thing I felt before he
levered himself away was the lustiness of his desire.

He stood before me with his hands by his sides,
his weight on one hip and his head bowed. It was a
minute before I returned to earth enough to realize
how far gone I'd been. Looking up at that bowed
head, knowing that if he'd backed me into the living
room and lowered me to the sofa, I'd probably have
been the one to reach for his belt, I didn't know what
to say.

After all I'd said about loving Adam and not wanting to be involved with another man, I'd put on quite
a show. He'd have been right to call me a fraud.

He wasn't calling me anything, though, but continued to silently stand there with his head hung low,
while the pace of his breathing gradually slowed.
Only then did he lift his gaze to mine.

"I have to leave," he said. The lingering thread of
hoarseness in his voice was the only remnant of passion. Though his eyes were as compelling as ever, the
sexual drive that had darkened their spokes was gone.
"See ya."

With neither a smile nor a touch nor a single other
word, he left me at the door, walked straight to his
car, climbed in, backed around and drove off.

I watched in disbelief, waiting for him to step on
the brake, roll down his window and call out something sweet like, "I'll phone you tonight," or, "Take
care of yourself until I get back," or, "Wow, what a
kiss!" But he didn't stop. The Saab continued on
down my drive, rounded a curve and disappeared. By
that time, I'd run to the side of the house and had my

eyes glued to that curve. I held my breath and waited. I blinked. My mouth dropped open.

"See ya?" I murmured dazedly, then, "See ya!" After a second, I put my hands on my hips and cried, "*See ya!* Is that all you have to say after what just happened? You kiss me to oblivion, put your hands all over me, and all you have to say is, *See ya?*" I whirled around and stormed back to the house. "You are a first class *jerk*, Peter Hathaway. No wonder you've never been married. No woman will *have* you. Women don't want a man who takes what he can get and then pulls on his boots and says—" I dropped my voice to imitate Peter's "—See ya." My voice shot up again. "Goodbye and good *riddance*," I yelled to the wind. Stalking inside, I gave the old oak door a mighty shove.

"Who does he think he is?" I muttered. I paced in a small circle, gesturing with my hand as I ranted, "Who does he think *I* am? A princess—hah! The Madigan heiress—*hah!* Does he think I'm made of stone? Does he think I turn myself on and off like a faucet? Doesn't he know I'm human? Doesn't he know what he's done to me?" Feeling suddenly deflated, I stopped pacing and stood in the middle of the floor. I saw nothing but shades of bleakness. In a weak voice I said, "Doesn't he know what I've done to myself?"

My legs wobbled. I sank to the floor, pulling my knees to my chest and cinching them in with my arms. Then I buried my face and cried.

6

I recovered, of course. It wasn't often that I resorted to tears, but when I did, they were marvelously cathartic. By the time I wiped my eyes and rose from the floor, I'd decided that the life I'd shaped for myself over the years was too strong to be shadowed for long by something as ephemeral as desire, particularly when other shadows loomed darker.

With Peter's departure, the pall of Cooper's dilemma settled over me again. On the one hand, I felt better having hired Peter; for whatever else I might begrudge the man, his competence had never been an issue. Knowing that he was back in New York working on Cooper's behalf was a comfort. On the other hand, I was frustrated. I wanted to do more. I wanted to take an active part in Cooper's defense. I wanted to find out who had set him up.

The problem was how to do it. I thought about it a lot over the next few days, and when I wasn't thinking about it, I was swept up in my work. Between the two, my mind was constantly busy. I didn't leave myself time to think about Peter Hathaway or his kiss or his "See ya."

The potting went well. By the first of the week, I had completed three new pieces that I felt Moni would love. As always before a show, I'd been worried. But with those pieces done, my worries eased. The ball was rolling. I felt reasonably confident that I'd be able to produce more than enough to make the show different.

In keeping with my determination to stay on Cooper's case, I spent Tuesday morning with Benjie Drake. He was the one member of the crew whom Peter hadn't had much of a crack at, and though I knew Benjie hadn't had anything to do with the smuggling itself, I wasn't putting it past him to have seen or heard something that he took upon himself to judge insignificant.

He wasn't thrilled that I'd stopped by. "Cooper's not here," he said. He spared me only a cursory glance as I walked into the kitchen, where he was in the process of fixing some sort of drink that looked suspiciously like a hangover remedy, which made sense, seeing as he looked suspiciously hung over.

"That's okay. I thought you and I could talk."

"About what?"

"Cooper. The boat. The crew."

He was silent for a good, long time, during which he stood at the counter with his back to me and one hand on his hip, and forced down the concoction he'd made. Studying him from the rear, I had to admit that he was well built. Only an inch or two shy of Cooper's height, he had the same wedge-shaped body, the same hard lines. I could see why girls panted after him, though, personally, I preferred more maturity in a frame. Cooper's body had that maturity, a fullness that spoke of time and life and love. Peter's had it even more, along with a sexiness the other two lacked. But then, like beauty, sexiness was in the eye of the beholder.

I was a beholder when it came to Peter.

Miffed at the thought, I settled into a chair at the table, scowled at Benjie's back and waited. My scowl faded. Eventually, he turned.

He looked like hell. Forget the wrinkled jeans and shirt that he'd clearly slept in. Forget the stubble on his face and the redness in his eyes. His expression was a world-weary one, far too old for his years.

"What about them?" he asked in a disgruntled tone.

"He's in trouble, Benjie." We both knew I was talking of Cooper. "He's in trouble, and if we don't come up with something, he could go to prison."

"He won't. That New York dude'll keep him out."

"Peter isn't a miracle worker. The fact is that those stolen diamonds were found in Cooper's possession." I wanted to impress that on him; I wasn't sure if he understood its significance. "That's like getting caught with your hand in the till. It's hard to say you're innocent when they catch you that way." I paused. Either Benjie was unaffected by what I was saying, or his mind was on hold. His face looked blank.

"Maybe I should come back another time." I started to get up.

"Don't. Say what you have to."

What he was thinking, I knew, was *Get it over with, then get out and leave me alone.* What *I* was thinking was that Benjie didn't deserve Cooper, but then, it wasn't the first time I'd thought it. On the one hand, I wanted to like Benjie. I wanted to be compassionate. The kid had lost his parents in a tragic way, and even before that his life had been hard. It was sad that he acted out, sad that he thought getting drunk was macho, sad that he wasn't in therapy.

But damn it, it was sad only to a point. Past that point, it was hard finding compassion for a boy—man—who seemed without a drop of it for anyone else, least of all his own brother.

I contemplated leaving, simply to be free of Benjie, who set me on edge each time I was with him. Then I thought of Cooper's predicament and settled back in the chair.

"I was saying," I repeated, quite willing to drill it into Benjie's head, "that the diamonds were found in Cooper's cabin. Someone obviously put them there."

"You already know what I think," Benjie said and turned around to drag an opened bag of potato chips from the shelf.

"He was framed. But by whom? And why? You work on the boat, Benjie. Do you think it was one of the others?"

"How should I know?" he mumbled through a mouthful of chips.

"You should know because you work with them."

"So does Cooper. Does he know?"

"He says he'll vouch for each of them."

Benjie's mouth twisted dryly. "Smart Cooper," he muttered under his breath.

"What's that supposed to mean?"

He shrugged. "That he knows. If he says they're innocent, they're innocent."

I decided to overlook his sarcasm. "Maybe not. Maybe there are some things he doesn't see. Maybe there are some things you can see that Cooper, being captain of the boat, can't see."

"I doubt it." He shoved more chips into his mouth.

"Think, Benjie. Think."

"You think I haven't?" He chewed fast, then swallowed. I could see that he was angry, but if his anger produced even the slightest clue, it was worth it. "What do you want me to do—pull something out of thin air just to give you someone to blame? You love Cooper. In your eyes, he's perfect. You'd probably be happy to pin this on *anyone* else just to clear him."

"I want the guilty party found. That's all."

"And then what? You'll drum it into Cooper's head that you've saved his life, so he'll be forever beholden to you? He won't marry you, y'know. He won't ever marry you."

I was taken aback by the venom in his tone. It sounded as though he hated me, but I couldn't imagine why. Okay, so we'd never been the best of friends, and that had created some tension because Cooper and I *were* the best of friends. But Benjie and I had never come to blows. I closely guarded the feelings I had about him, so that no one but Swansy—and now Peter—knew them. I'd never shared them with Cooper. I would never bad-mouth Benjie to him.

Rather than take the defensive and argue that Benjie's reasoning was all wrong, I said, "Of course,

Cooper won't marry me—any more than I'd marry him.''

"Bullshit. You'd marry him if he asked, but he won't ask."

"You sound like you two have discussed it."

"We don't have to. I have eyes. I see what Cooper's feeling and what he isn't. I'm not *that* dense, Jill."

"I never thought you were dense. All I thought was that maybe something happened on the boat, something that seemed perfectly normal at the time but that in hindsight could be looked at a different way." I held up a hand. I didn't want to fight, not with Benjie, who was just then more boy than man. "Okay. For the sake of discussion, we'll assume that the crew of the *Free Reign* is innocent. We know that the diamonds had to have been stowed in Cooper's cabin while the boat was docked at Grand Bank, since that was the only stop she made. Who could have done it?"

He looked at me as though I were the dense one. "Any one of a hundred people who were walkin' around the docks."

"Did you notice anyone paying an unusual amount of attention to the *Free Reign*?"

"Sure. There was a waitress at a lunch place right there. We went out the first night. She couldn't take her eyes off the boat after that. Couldn't get enough of catching looks at me. I know, 'cause I watched her, too." He cupped his hands in front of his chest and grinned. "Great pair of jugs."

I made a face. "That's disgusting."

He looked at my breasts. "Yours aren't bad, either." The grin vanished when his eyes rose. "But it doesn't mean a thing to Cooper. He wouldn't give a damn what kind of boobs you got. He's not interested."

Unable to help myself, I cried, "Benjie, what's *with* you? Why are you so hung up on my relationship with Cooper? I *know* he's not interested in me, either for marrying or for sex, and I'm not interested in him those ways, either. If you think I'm going to barge in and steal some of his attention away from you, you can relax. I won't do that. I'm no threat to you." It seemed absurd that he'd think I was. If he'd been ten, or twelve or fifteen, I might have bought it. But at twenty?

Tossing the bag of chips to the counter, he tugged open the refrigerator, took out a half-gallon bottle of milk, put it to his mouth and drank. My first thought was that it was going to spill all over him. My second thought, when it didn't, was that he was obviously practiced in drinking that way. My third thought was that it was a pretty unsanitary thing to do. My fourth thought was that it wasn't my job to tell him.

Wearing a ridiculous white mustache over his dark stubble, he looked at me and said, "I never thought you were a threat. More like a pest. You butted in where you didn't belong. Cooper was doin' just fine with McHenry."

"Wrong. McHenry is a local lawyer who does just fine when the charge is disturbing the peace or driving to endanger. Smuggling of stolen goods is a little over his head." I paused. "But I thought you had confidence in Peter. You said before that he'd get him off.''

''Sure, he will. So would McHenry if you'd left him alone.'' None too gently, he returned the milk to the fridge. ''Cooper isn't as helpless as you think. And he isn't alone. He has people b'side you to take care of him.''

''I'm glad to hear it,'' I said and pushed myself to my feet. Benjie wasn't going to tell me anything new, and I'd had enough of him for one day. ''Thanks for the warning, Benj.'' I headed for the door. ''I'll make sure that I don't set myself up for a fall where Cooper's concerned.''

I was halfway out the door when Benjie's voice followed. ''You don't have to be sarcastic—''

Gently but firmly, I closed the door.

That run-in with Benjie—and it could only be called that—bothered me. I didn't mention it to Swansy at first, because I thought maybe I was making something out of nothing. Benjie had always been contrary. He wasn't really behaving out of character—except for those references to Cooper and me. He'd never made them before. I wondered why he did now.

Obviously it had to do with the case, but I wasn't sure which part. Was it the case itself, or Peter's involvement in it, or something as simple as my presence in his kitchen when he wanted to be alone? Fragments of his thoughts kept echoing in my mind, unsettling me enough so that by the time Friday rolled around, I was ready to talk.

*   *   *

"It's infuriating," I told Swansy soon after I arrived. "Cooper shouldn't be going through this, and given the fact that he is, Benjie shouldn't be adding to his grief. What's the matter with that boy?"

"He's a victim of circumstance."

"I know that, and I try to be gentle, but it's hard. He doesn't like me."

"You're smarter 'n he is, so you make him nervous."

I shook my head. "He thinks I'm going to come between Cooper and him. I told him I'd never do that."

Swansy was silent. She gave me that gentle smile of hers that urged me on. I fell easy prey to it.

"He thinks I have designs on Cooper. Serious designs—like marriage. Isn't that a hoot? Cooper and me and marriage? Forget the me part. Cooper and marriage? Somehow I don't associate the two."

She remained silent.

"Why is that?" I asked. "There've never been starbursts between Cooper and me, but why not with someone else? He's a special guy. He doesn't say much. He takes a little getting to know, but once you do he has so much to offer."

"He doesn't think so."

"That's crazy."

"Sometimes people have reasons for bein' crazy."

"What are Cooper's?"

She was quiet for such a long time that I was about to speak myself, when she said, "He had a sweetheart once. Maybe he still loves her."

My eyes went wide. I sat forward. "Who?" But Swansy wasn't about to tell, and I knew it. She wasn't a gossip. She dropped hints of secrets here and there only when she felt there was a need for it. In this case, the need had to do with my understanding Cooper better. The identity of the woman wasn't important, simply that there'd been one once upon a time.

"Cooper and a sweetheart," I murmured. "Interesting." Many times I'd pictured Cooper's women, the ones he went to for sex. I'd never pictured a sweetheart, though, one he went to for love. "Does Benjie know about her?" It would explain his utter conviction that Cooper would never marry me.

"It was a long time ago."

"Where is she now?" I asked. Swansy didn't answer. "Did she marry someone else?" Still no answer. "She must have. Otherwise she'd have been with Cooper."

"If she loved him."

Oh dear. Cooper had loved her, but she hadn't loved him back. The hurt I felt for him quickly turned to anger. "She was a fool, then, a fool. Men like Cooper don't come along every day."

"T'hear you talk, you'd think you were in love with him yourself, girl."

"I do love him, but not in that way. I respect him. I admire him. It's not that he has great ambitions, or that he's some kind of superstar, but in his everyday existence, he's an eminently capable man."

Swansy gave a slow, thoughtful nod but didn't say a word.

"Adam wasn't." I remembered our lives together.

"Poor Adam. He was a dreamer far more than a doer. We were both so excited about leaving home. I'd had it with my family, and he'd had it with his."

"Real different, your families."

"But just as stressful. In my case it was social pressure as in materialism, jealousy and spite. In his case, it was an obsession with upward mobility. His family was where mine was two generations ago. They kept pushing Adam, pushing him to do better in school, to earn more money each summer, to befriend this executive's son or that politician's daughter. When he told them he was going to be a fisherman, they went nuts."

Swansy sat very still.

I hung my head. "Maybe they were right." Dark thoughts filled my mind. "Adam wasn't an athlete. He wasn't physically coordinated. Aside from his height and weight, he was the most improbable of fishermen. Without Cooper, he'd never have made it as long as he did." The darkness deepened. My voice came from a tortured spot deep inside. "I kept telling him he could do it, that he could do anything he wanted. I thought I was doing the right thing." The memory tormented me. "If I hadn't pushed, he'd have given up. And if he'd done that, he'd be alive today."

"Stop that, girl! It's not your fault he's dead. He went on the boat of his own free will, and an accident happened. They do sometimes, y'know."

"But fishing?" My eyes flew to her face. "He shouldn't have been fishing in the first place. It was a misplaced dream, a romantic notion that just didn't fit him. He hated fishing. In the end, he really hated it.''

''So why didn't he stop?''

''Because I kept encouraging him to go on.''

''And he wasn't man enough to stand up to you?''

The suggestion hit me like a slap in the face. I opened my mouth to deny it, then closed it again and swallowed hard.

Swansy started rocking. The gently creaking rhythm of the runners on the floor soothed my ruffled thoughts.

I took a deep, uneven breath. ''I loved him.''

Swansy patted my knee. ''Yes, you did, girl. You loved him a whole lot. He was lucky. Had more love in three years than some men have in a lifetime.''

That thought stuck with me for a long time after I left her house. Cooper was certainly one of those men who'd missed out, but as the weekend came and went, I found myself wondering where Peter stood on that score.

Then I wondered why I cared. He hadn't called—at least, he hadn't called me. He'd called Cooper several times to ask questions and update him on what was going on, but as far as I knew, he hadn't bothered to ask how I was.

It was infuriating.

I vented that fury on my work, which meant that the pieces I produced as the days passed were darker and more dramatic than the rest of the collection. That didn't worry me. They were still good. Actually they were better than good, I decided. The more I looked at them the better they seemed. And I spent hours doing that. They intrigued me.

Without doubt, they were more sensual than anything I'd done before. Sensual, sexual, erotic. Absurd as it seemed to refer to pottery in those terms, they were the ones that consistently came to mind. The joining of a handle to a pitcher, the curve of the neck of a decanter, the undulation of the sides of a decorative bowl—I stared long and hard. And much of the time I wondered whether I was seeing something in them that no one else would see.

It wasn't only in my work that I was seeing things sensual, sexual and erotic. My nights were filled with them. I'd never had an X-rated dream in my life, yet suddenly they were coming in a steady procession. At least once, sometimes twice a night I awoke flushed and damp, with a tingling in my breasts and belly and a throbbing between my legs.

Once, the experience would have been embarrassing. Over and over, it was mortifying. I could only thank my lucky stars that there was no one in my bed to witness the folly.

Then again, I supposed that the folly wouldn't be at all, if there was someone in my bed.

I was hungry, and *he*'d done it. *His* face was the one atop the body that loomed over mine each night. *His* mouth was the one that muffled my fevered cries. *His* hands were the ones that brought me to sanity's edge.

Still he didn't call.

So I called my mother. It was on a Wednesday night, three weeks to the day since Peter had gone.

"Hi, Mom," I breezed, as though my call were a regular thing. "How's everything?"

"Jillian? Jillian? Is that you calling me, Jillian?"

There had never been, nor would there ever be anything wrong with my mother's hearing. Nor was there anything wrong with mine. I could clearly hear the facetious tongue in her cheek. I let out a breath. "Yes, Mom. It's me."

"What's wrong?"

"Nothing's wrong."

"Are you well?"

"Very well."

"Are you sure?"

"Yes."

"Then you must be calling about Peter."

My mother had always been unusually perceptive. Growing up with her, I'd appreciated it at times— when I first got my period and was too embarrassed to tell her, for example, or several years later, when I refused to visit family friends whose oldest son had all but raped me the last time we'd visited.

Her perceptiveness had a down side, though. She could see through me easily, so early on, I'd stopped trying to hide my feelings.

But that wasn't to say that I never tried again.

"No, Mom, I'm not calling about Peter. There's nothing much to say about him."

"Are you pleased with his work?"

"He seems to be on top of things," I told her with what I thought was just the right amount of indifference. "The trial is set to start in three months. He has a lot of work to do between now and then."

"If his reputation stands, he'll do it."

"I hope so." In truth, I had no doubt about it, but feigning doubt helped my cause. "I worry a little that Cooper may be a small fish in a big pond. We may be in trouble if Peter has something else going on."

"Of course he has other things going on. No lawyer can support himself on one case."

"I know, but what if a *spectacular* case came along. It would overshadow everything else."

"Do you have reason to think that's happened?"

I hesitated. "No."

"But you're wondering if I've heard anything. No, Jillian, to my knowledge he hasn't fallen across anything *spectacular* since he agreed to represent your friend."

That meant he had no spectacular reason for not having called me. I sighed. "That's a relief. I was worried."

"Frankly," my mother said—unnecessarily, because she was always frank—"I'm surprised you to have to ask me. That's the kind of question you have every right to ask him yourself, since you're paying him so much money. You should have asked it at the time you retained him."

"It didn't seem necessary then. He spent five full days here. He wouldn't have been able to do that if he'd had anything of a spectacular nature going on back home. I was just wondering if anything's come up since, and the reason I haven't asked is that Cooper is the one who talks with him most."

"Cooper?"

"Yes, Mom. Cooper. You know, my friend Cooper, who is accused of—"

"But why is Cooper doing the talking?"

"Because that's the way it should be. Cooper's the defendant."

"I want *you* to talk with Peter. I want *you* to get to know him."

"Why is that, Mom?"

"Oh, *please*, Jillian. Must I spell it out?"

She didn't have to. I knew just what she was going to say, but I wanted to hear her say it anyway. "Yes."

She gave a sigh that seemed to convey the years of frustration I'd single-handedly caused her. "What am I going to do with you, Jillian? There are times when I wonder where your mind is—but I do know where it is. It's up there in that godforsaken old house you have on that godforsaken cliff. I felt a glimmer of hope when you called for the name of a lawyer for your friend. It was clearly the right thing to do. I thought that maybe your mind was beginning to work again. But it isn't. It's atrophying up there. If you can't even see that Peter Hathaway is husband material, you're a lost cause."

"Husband material for whom?" I asked, all innocence.

"*You!* Who else would I be concerned about!"

"But he must have dozens of women in the city," I remarked, then held my breath and prayed that Mom was just riled up enough to lack her usual perception.

My luck held up. She sounded indignant. "If he had dozens of women in the city, I'd never be pushing him on you. No daughter of mine needs used goods, *particularly* in this day and age. There's so much going around! That's *all* we need.''

''It only takes one contact with the wrong woman to do the damage.''

''The man is very careful, Jillian. I checked that out before I ever called you with his name.''

''What do you mean, you checked it out? How can you check out something like that?''

''I know people. I know people who know people, and one of those people knows an old flame of Peter's. It seems he's a one-woman man. He doesn't run with the crowd the way some of them still do, AIDS or no AIDS. He had a long-term relationship with this particular woman, and before that there was a long-term relationship with another woman.''

''And before that another one? How about after? What's he been doing with himself since that old flame friend of your friend?''

''He dates casually. Nothing more.''

''Does he use condoms?'' I asked, thinking how far I'd come from the day I couldn't tell my mother I'd gotten my period.

''Good Lord, Jillian, how would I know something like that?''

''You know everything else.''

''Not everything. I don't know for sure why none of those relationships ever ended in marriage.'' She grew pensive. ''I do wonder about that. It's surprising that, successful as he is, he doesn't want a family.''

''He's in his prime. He has time.''

''Still, it's better to have children when you're younger. Look at your father and me. We were just out of school. Our children are grown now, but we're still young enough to lead active, exciting lives."

I wanted to remind her that they'd led active, exciting lives even when we'd been kids. Money could buy whatever child care was needed. That didn't mean the children always benefitted from the arrangement, but it did permit their parents to lead active, exciting lives.

I fantasized differently about Peter. "Maybe he wants to wait to have children until he's at a stage in his career when he can afford to be an active father. Men are doing that nowadays."

"Do you think he'd make a good father?"

I'd thought about that. "I don't know. Several times when he was up here, there were kids around. He didn't go ga-ga over them. But he wasn't bothered by them. If anything, he seemed a little shy. I suppose it's understandable. He had an older brother who left home early on, but there were no younger siblings. He's had no experience with kids."

"Does that bother you?"

"Why would it? I'm no more experienced than he is."

"If you were to have children, one of you should know what you're doing."

"We'd learn pretty quick." Only after the words were out did I realize what I'd said. I'd stepped right into it. Once a shrewd defense attorney, my mother hadn't lost her touch. "Hypothetically, of course. Neither of us is planning on having children, least of all together."

"You've discussed it?"

"Of course not!" I couldn't believe how quickly I'd lost my advantage in the discussion. Taking a slow breath, I went on more calmly. "My relationship with Peter is professional. Much as I hate to disappoint you, we didn't fall in love at first sight."

"Maybe you will on second sight, or third."

"Not likely. I'm not interested in falling in love again."

Mom gave one of those wise laughs that I hated. They usually preceded a truism. This time was no exception. "I'm sorry to be the one to tell you this, Jillian, because you don't usually believe what I say, but love happens sometimes whether we want it or not."

"Not to me," I insisted. "I'm very much in control of what is and is not going on in my life."

"Then why did you call, if not to pump me on what I knew about Peter Hathaway's social life?"

"I called," I told her, sounding remarkably mature and unruffled, given that she had me pegged, "to tell you I've decided to go to the show in New York. You're on the mailing list, so you'll be getting a notice with the details, but it's on for the second week in November. The opening is on Sunday afternoon, but there's going to be a pre-opening thing the Friday evening before. You're all invited to that, if you want to come," I knew they wouldn't, "or if you want to stop by during the regular times. I was thinking maybe you'd take the train up and we'd meet for lunch one day."

"Do you have to be at the show the whole time?"

"I should be, since I've decided to go."

"But do you have to?"

"Not necessarily."

"Then why not come home for one of those nights? I'll invite everyone over. We can have a nice family dinner together." She paused, and I could just see one elegant brow arching. "Unless you were planning to be home for Thanksgiving anyway."

I wasn't, and she knew it. I had hoped that one or more members of my family coming into New York, which they did often enough, would eliminate my need to go to Philadelphia. But my shows didn't appeal to the Madigans, and I could see why. If my work was being shown at the Guggenheim, they'd have been there in a minute. The Fletcher-Dunn Gallery was something else. *I* found it exciting, because the patrons of the gallery appreciated the kind of work I was doing, though it wouldn't bother me if I never had a show, and I certainly didn't aspire to the Guggenheim.

One part of me thought it was too bad that my family couldn't recognize my career by putting in an appearance at my show. The other part was just as happy to keep them separate from my work. So if I had to go to Philadelphia, I supposed I could.

"How does Monday night sound?" I asked.

"Off the top of my head, it sounds fine," Mom answered. "I'll check with everyone here. If there's a problem, I'll let you know."

"If I don't hear from you, then, I'll give you a call when I get to New York. I'll be making reservations at the Park Lane."

"The Park Lane? Why the Park Lane, when your

father can get you a suite at the Parker Meridien for next to nothing?''

''The Park Lane is fine for what I want,'' I told her. I didn't like taking favors from my father's friends, because the favors almost always involved a catch, and I didn't want to owe anyone a thing. Besides, I liked the Park Lane. It was on Central Park South. ''Take care, Mom. I'll talk with you soon.''

I pressed the button on my phone, then released it and punched out Moni's number in New York. I wanted to tell her that I'd decided to attend the show. I also wanted her to make the hotel reservations for me, and to see that an invitation to the pre-opening reception was sent to Peter.

After all, he was my best friend's lawyer, on retainer to me. And he lived in New York. If nothing else, he could fill me in on the latest developments in Cooper's case.

7

Cooper's case was the last thing on my mind as November progressed and the show drew near. The first thing on my mind was work. I was determined to give Moni everything she'd asked for and more, which meant that I spent most of my waking hours in the studio.

Of course, I still made time for Swansy and Cooper and the others who were so dear to me. Seeing them each day, being part of their lives was as important to me as my work. They needed me, and being needed was a vital part of my makeup. It was one of the main things that had been missing in my old life, where people's needs for each other were selfish, usually material and almost always fickle. Adam had come along with an emotional need that I'd filled to a tee. We'd moved here, and I'd found that in my own small way I could fill the needs of even more people. Even after Adam died, the sense of fulfillment remained.

In fact given that satisfaction, I wasn't quite sure why I was working so hard for this show. I hadn't done it for either of the other two shows I'd had. Shows didn't impress me, certainly not with my own skill as a potter. I potted for the creative outlet it gave me. Yes, I enjoyed seeing my finished product and improving on it next time, but I'd have been just as happy to sell in the small crafts shops that dotted New England as to sell in New York. There were times when I rued the day Moni had seen my work in that Kennebunkport shop.

The thing was, I didn't want my career to run away with itself so that I lost the simple pleasure of potting. So I was very careful, very careful as I spent hours in that attic in preparation for this show, and I would have stopped at the first feeling of drudgery.

It never came. I had all the energy in the world, along with a drive that surprised me. I wanted this show to be the best I'd had so far, and I was willing to invest the time and energy to make it so.

The drive lasted until three days before I was to leave for New York. I'd finished everything I'd be showing. Cooper had helped me crate the pieces. He and Norman Gudeau, the local boy I hired, had loaded the crates on a U-Haul, and Norman had set off for New York.

There wasn't much left for me to do but pack, and there wasn't much of that to do because I'd decided to fly down a day early to shop. I was free to do nothing but think about the trip.

That was when I was forced to admit to the source of my energy. With no other outlet, I thought about Peter, and when I thought about him, I thought about sex. The excitement I'd felt when I'd been working with clay remained with me, only now I knew it to be anticipation. My heart caught more times each day than I cared to count, and the tingles that began with those catches, then spread through my limbs before retracing their routes and gatherings in a low coil of need in the pit of my stomach, could only be called arousal.

I was a fool, I told myself. Peter wasn't interested in me. If he were, he would have called, but he hadn't done that once. He called Cooper regularly, but I hadn't heard his voice since that last, despicable, "See ya." And I had no cause to expect that I'd see him in New York. Just because Moni dropped him an invitation to my show didn't mean he would put in an appearance. I intended to call him while I was there, purely on a professional basis, of course, but a phone call wasn't a face-to-face visit.

And I craved a face-to-face visit as I'd never craved anything before.

I fantasized. I fantasized about what he'd look like wearing city gear, then what he'd look like wearing nothing. I fantasized about lying naked on his bed, watching him approach with that tight-hipped walk of his, only I'd see his hips in the flesh, I'd see his flat belly and his thighs and the dark thatch of hair from which would jut the promise of my relief.

At times the strength of my fantasies appalled me. In an attempt to dispel them, I wandered through the house trying to remember things that Adam and I had done in each of the rooms. But the memories had faded. They were sweet, cherished in corners of my mind and heart like roses that had been pressed in a scrapbook years before. Like those roses, their smell was gone, as was the soft, velvety feel of their petals and the richness of their color. They couldn't begin to compete with the heat and vibrancy of my fantasies.

With orgasmic pacing, those fantasies came and went in waves. When they ebbed, I could function as I'd done for so long before Peter entered my life. When they began their surge, though, I was without the control I'd always prided myself on. Nothing seemed to help, least of all remembering Adam. Something stronger had taken me over. I was in its grip, as surely as Adam had been taken by the sea.

It was worse at night, early in the morning, late in the afternoon. More than one dusk found me walking out on the bluff, then sitting atop a boulder and hugging my legs tightly together. The cool November wind whipped through my hair, slapped my heated cheeks, buffeted my huddled form, but the relief I sought wasn't there. The sea was Adam, yet it wasn't Adam's ghost that swayed with the tide, taunting me by coming and going, coming and going.

You could do with a good tumble, Cooper had said, and he was right. The screaming need in me was a physical one. A man's possession would do the trick. Once. Just once. Then I could get on with my life.

When I hit New York on Thursday afternoon, it was every bit as bad as I'd always found it. The crowds bothered me. The traffic bothered me. The steady drone of mechanical noise, so different from the steady rhythm of the sea, bothered me.

What bothered me most, of course, was that Peter was out there, thinking about heaven only knew what, but not me. In typically female fashion—though I'd have screeched if someone had used those words to me—I took my frustration out in the stores. The sales-people didn't mind it a bit, but then, who would mind a bonanza in commissions?

I went from one to another of the small boutiques that over the years I'd come to know. By the time I was done with my spree, a bevy of shopping bags hung from my shoulders and elbows, and my ward-robe was richer by two suits, two dresses, a silk slacks-and-blouse outfit, shoes, stocking and hand-bags to match the finery, a pair of jeans, a hand-knit sweater and some of the sexiest underwear that I'd ever seen, much less bought. My final purchase was a huge canvas pouch to carry all the others home to Maine.

Every step of the way back to the hotel, I called myself ten kinds of fools. But I didn't stop and turn around. Nor did I consider returning what I'd bought.

Thursday evening, wearing one of those new dresses, I had dinner with Moni, and with Bill Fletcher and Celia Dunn, the owners of the gallery, who assured me, as Norman already had, that my pieces had arrived safely and were in the process of being put on display. I was pleased to hear that, but in a distracted sort of way. My thoughts were else-where.

I was back in my room by eleven, feeling the same insidious restlessness that had plagued me at home. Strangely, it was heightened by everything about the city. The life I'd chosen for myself was so different from this, and the crowds, the traffic, the noise made me feel removed from so much of what I'd been.

That was, I supposed, why I felt no guilt at the thought of the purchases I'd made that afternoon. It was also, I supposed, why first thing the next morning I phoned Samantha's hairdresser—Samantha *always* went into Manhattan to have her hair done—and took the space opened up by a ten o'clock cancellation. I didn't want my hair cut, just shaped and styled, and while I was at it, I had a facial, then a manicure and pedicure. One thing seemed to lead to the next. It had been a long time since I'd sat in a chair and let myself be pampered. I wasn't about to say that I'd have the patience to do it more than once in a great while. Still, it was nice. It made me feel feminine, and when I walked out of the place, I felt unusually attractive—all of which coordinated well with the feelings of sensuality that were a stirring brew in my belly.

Friday night's reception was scheduled for six-thirty, to catch all the budding young executives, male and female, before they headed out for the weekend. I was to be there by six, and for that I started dressing at four. I wanted to look just right. After all, if I'd gone to such an effort with clothes and hair and nails, I didn't want to blow the effect by putting myself together wrong.

I did just fine with my bath, which was lightly laced with jasmine-scented bath oils, courtesy of the Park Lane. I did just fine with a heavily laced silky white teddy, with a garter belt and sheer navy stockings. But when I began on my makeup, I ran into trouble, and it had nothing to do with a lack of practice.

My hands shook. They were obviously echoing the

tremors that rippled continuously through my insides, but that knowledge didn't help when it came to drawing the finest of navy lines under and over my lashes. The process took forever and involved several wipe offs and redos, which involved my lavender eye shadow as well. Then I had to repair the damage I did when I accidentally brushed mascara across the bridge of my nose. By the time I'd finished with faint strokes of blusher and focused on my lips, I settled for a simple peachy gloss, rather than something darker and more dramatic but harder to apply.

To this day, I'm not sure whether it would have been better or worse if I'd known Peter was coming. Not knowing for sure, I was frightened he wouldn't come. If I'd known he *was* coming, I'd have been all the more frightened by the possibilities. I needed him. My body needed his. The mere thought of it sent my temperature up a degree or two, and I wasn't thinking about much else so I was in a constant state of warmth.

In heat, so to speak.

When a last-minute case of the jitters struck, it was all I could do not to tear off silk, lace and makeup, throw on my jeans and take off for a hike through the park. But a woman didn't do that in New York. And I knew it wouldn't solve my problem. I'd tried fresh air and hiking back home, and it had done little to curb the desire that had taken root and was flourishing, like an exotic mushroom, in the dark, moist, feminine recesses of my body.

Gathering what composure I could, I finished dressing. My hair took little more than the flick of a brush to restore it to the condition in which Samantha's hairdresser had left it. The only jewelry I wore was a pair of large white enamel discs that were simple enough to complement rather than compete with my suit, the new one I'd bought for the occasion. It was of navy silk, with a petal skirt that hit the knee, a white blouse whose gently ruffled collar dipped low, and a jacket that was nipped in at the waist before flaring down six inches into the semblance of a bustle. With those sheer navy stockings, navy shoes and bag, I felt quite chic.

But shaky, damn it, shaky.

By the time I reached the gallery, I was thanking my lucky stars I'd been born a Madigan. If I looked cool and calm and together, it was only thanks to years of training under the most demanding of masters.

Stand straight, Jillian. Shoulders back. Chin level.

Look at the person you're talking with, Jillian. Let him think he's the most interesting one in the world.

Don't touch your hair. Don't touch your clothes. And whatever you do, Jillian, don't touch your face.

Smile gently, Jillian. We didn't spend thousands on orthodontia work to see you grimace.

Mother would have been proud if she'd been there. *I* was proud. As the invited guests—mostly people from the gallery's A-list, plus those who'd bought my pieces before—began to arrive, I moved around the room with Bill Fletcher, who knew them all. He introduced me to small groups at a time. Smiling my gentlest smile, I nodded my way around the faces, shook hands where hands were offered, answered questions about my work and about living in Maine. My life-style seemed to fascinate New Yorkers and was as good a conversational gambit as any. When wine was passed, I accepted a glass from Bill and managed to hold it remarkably steady. From time to time I sipped, but I wasn't any more eager to imbibe than I was to sample the hors d'oeuvres that were making the rounds.

The gallery meandered through three rooms, each at slightly different levels. Bill guided me along, passing me at one point to his partner, Celia Dunn, who took up the circulating where he'd left off. Though I would have liked to have stayed in the front room to monitor the new arrivals, that wasn't always possible. I was alert, though. Between gentle smiles and small talk, sometimes under the guise of considering a question that had been posed, I unobtusively scanned the heads in sight. Though my pulse raced in anticipation each time, there were never even any close calls. I knew what Peter looked like. No other man, regardless of how closely his height and coloring resembled Peter's, held himself quite the same way.

He arrived at seven-thirty. Incredibly, I felt his presence before I saw him, though whether it was wishful thinking that made my heart beat faster or extrasensory perception, I'll never know. We were in the innermost of the three rooms at the time. I had just finished telling a middle-aged couple from Westchester what it was like to work overlooking the ocean when I looked toward the door to the second room, and there he was.

His eyes met mine. I will never forget that first

moment of visual contact for as long as I live. My heart caught and held. The faces that separated us seemed to fade out, along with the sound and everything else about the room. We were alone with each other, and the fire in his eyes told of his desire.

"...artistry is intricately entwined with the tides, don't you think?" the female half of the couple was asking.

The sound of her voice shattered the walls of our private tunnel. I tore my eyes from Peter's and returned them to her, sucking in a surreptitious breath to put my lungs back to work. Since I couldn't begin to speak yet, I nodded and prayed she'd continue talking, which she did. That bought me a minute's recovery time.

It took far more than a minute. One didn't drop from heart-stopping heaven back down to earth with a snap of the fingers, or, in this case, a shift of the eyes. Peter's appearance had burned its way into me, raising my pulse, my heat, my awareness of myself as a woman. Since I couldn't make any of that go away now that he was in the room, I could only hope to control it until I was free to give it its head.

"...he worked in stone. Quite interesting work. Have you seen his things?"

"Uh, no. I'm hoping to, though," I said a bit breathlessly and darted a glance at Peter, who was winding his way around clusters of guests, coming closer, ever closer.

Celia, bless her soul, must have sensed my distraction, because she graciously took up the slack. "Mrs. Moncrieff works exclusively in clay. The approach is quite different from what it would be if she were working with stone, as is the practicality of the finished pieces. Her work has a unique feel to it.''

''I can see that,'' the woman said and turned, with her husband and Celia, to the display stand on her right.

Peter approached on her left, but he wasn't any more interested in my pottery than I was. His eyes were riveted to mine. After pausing for a second on the outskirts of our group, he closed the small distance between us, slid an arm around my waist and brought me into a close hug.

Unable to help myself, I gave a tiny moan of relief. I was right back up there in heaven, sent there by the feel of his large, hard body against mine, the pressure of the arm that held me to him, the clean scent of soap and man, and the heat, oh, the heat. It was as sexual as heat got and radiated from him the way I supposed it was radiating from me. But what sent me to an even higher plane was the knowledge that he'd come.

He bent his dark head and pressed a warm kiss on my cheek, then eased me back and said in a low, rough rumble, ''Good to see you, Jill.''

In the eyes of the world, we were simply old friends, good friends. Though his hand lingered on my waist a bit longer than was necessary, it dropped to his side when Celia returned to us. He stayed close enough, though, so that by dropping my own hand, I could link my fingers with his in the shadow of my skirt.

I introduced him to Celia. She immediately recognized his name and was genuinely delighted that he'd stopped by, but before she could say much, Bill approached with a new group for a new round of introductions. With an effort I maintained my outward composure, smiling sweetly, talking rationally. All the while my stomach fluttered in response to the large man by my side.

Not about to let him run off with a stupid "See ya," I held tightly to his hand, but even in spite of that, he showed no sign of wanting to leave. He stood close, his shoulder backing mine, and he remained very much in the wings as though to profess that this was my night.

I began to wish that it wasn't. What I wanted to do was to go somewhere private with Peter, but the reception was slated to last until nine, and being the guest of honor, I couldn't very well disappear. At one point, under the guise of using the ladies' room, I excused myself and led Peter into Bill's office. The door had barely clicked behind us, blotting out the noise of the gallery, when he pressed me against it and captured my mouth.

There was nothing gentle about his kiss. It contained a fierce hunger that wasn't about to be contained. While his lips ground into mine, twisting and turning them to his will, his tongue ravished the inside of my mouth with deep, rhythmic thrusts.

Neither the kiss, nor its fierce hunger was one-sided. The fever in me had been building, craving just this outlet. Anchoring my hands in his hair to hold him close, I fought for my own satisfaction. My mouth was never still. At times it worked in counterpoint to his, at times in direct opposition, and though there was near violence in what we did, neither of us was close to being sated when a discreet knock came at the door.

"Oh Lord," Peter whispered. Pressing his forehead to mine, he dragged in a harsh breath.

My own breath was coming in short, sharp gasps that had as much to do with my arousal as with my frustration at having been interrupted. I didn't let go of his hair.

The knock came again.

Peter let out another, "Oh Lord." Pressing a light, moist kiss on my lips, he dragged my hands from the back of his head down his shoulders and over his shirt. He flattened them on his middle. "Later," he whispered, and his luminescent green eyes held the fire that promised more, far more of what we'd just shared.

I was thankful to be leaning against the door, because that look did nothing to still my quivering thighs. If anything, the fire inside burned hotter than it had before that kiss. My own look must have told Peter as much, because he swore softly, squeezed his eyes shut and bowed his head. After several seconds of utter silence, he straightened, bodily removed me from the door and opened it.

"Is Jill all right?" Moni asked. "I saw her head this way."

"She's fine. Just needed a break." He turned to me and asked in a low, gritty voice, "All set?"

With a nod I let him return me to the party, but I didn't let him move far from my side. He'd made me a promise behind the closed door of that office, and I intended to make him keep it. That knowledge was the only thing that made the burning inside me bearable.

Nine o'clock was forever in coming. I should have enjoyed those moments of glory, and if the circumstances had been different, I might have. People complimented me on my work, on my suit, on my choice of gallery, on Moni, and while I hadn't become a potter with an ego trip in mind, I wasn't immune to flattery.

Nevertheless, I couldn't appreciate it or anything else in that gallery except the tall, lean, hard-muscled man who stood by my side. So the minutes crept. I couldn't eat; I couldn't drink. I nodded and smiled and carried on chit-chat, but all the while my mind raced ahead to the satisfaction that waited. There were times when my cheeks grew crimson with my thoughts, and times when the cause for my smiles would have shocked those who received them if they'd known the truth. Every so often I was so distracted that I missed a question. Peter helped me out then, providing the answer requested while he warned me awake with a touch to my arm, my waist, my hand. Of course, those touches were counterproductive; they only sent me off again. But the effort was sweet.

He apparently had greater self-control than I did, though I suppose that was imperative. The male of the species had it harder—no pun intended. If he was aroused, it showed.

Conversely, I could be—and was—in a state of

sexual readiness with no one the wiser. No one could see that my insides were hot and achy, or that the sensitive flesh at the apex of my thighs was moist and swollen. Peter knew, of course, and that turned me on all the more. The minutes dragged until we could be alone.

Nine o'clock found us talking with a trio of latecomers. I was ready to swear they'd shown up purely for the sake of the wine and hors d'oeuvres; they didn't seem particularly interested in my work. But then, I wasn't particularly interested in my work, either.

Peter looked at his watch.

I smiled at the trio. "Will you excuse us?"

They did, of course. I led Peter through those others of the guests who lingered. When I found Moni, I leaned close and without pretense asked, "When can we leave?"

She shot a glance at Peter, then eyed me smugly. "I'd be in a rush, too, if I had him."

I bit my lip. I didn't want to be rude, but the hunger within me had reached a fever pitch. Having struggled to cope for the better part of the evening, I'd just about run out of smiles.

Mercifully, Moni seemed to realize that. But her smugness gave way to the concern of a friend. "Will you be okay?" she whispered. She didn't look at Peter again, but I knew she was thinking that she'd been the one to urge me to come to New York for the show, and in that sense I was her responsibility.

I didn't want to be anyone's responsibility but Peter's. "I'll be fine," I whispered back. I squeezed her hand and turned to leave, but her hand did a turn-around on mine to stay me.

"Are you sure?"

"Very sure. Very sure, Moni. I'll call you later tomorrow." This time she didn't hold me up. Peter went for my coat, while I said goodbye to Bill and Celia as graciously as I could in as little time as possible.

Moments later, Peter and I were half-walking, half-running toward Park Avenue, where we caught a cab.

"Your place or mine?" he asked in a thick voice.

I leaned toward the cabbie. "The Park Lane, please." As I sat back, Peter's hands framed my face—not so much to hold me still, I felt, but to anchor himself—and his mouth covered mine. A single touch was all it took. Like an explosion waiting to happen, a myriad of sensations rocked my body. I gasped into his mouth, then choked out a tiny cry when he filled mine with his tongue.

Needing an anchor of my own, I pushed my hands inside his coat, inside his suit jacket and, palms flat, over the firmly muscled planes of his pinpoint-cotton-covered chest. I ended up clasping his sides for the support that I needed. The world seemed to be spinning out of control around me.

We kissed with the desperation of lovers who needed to be naked and in bed, not fully dressed in the back seat of a cab. I wanted Peter to touch me, to touch me all over, but not once did his hands fall farther than my neck. It occurred to me that he did it deliberately, knowing that he'd lose control if he allowed himself greater liberty. But that reasoning was small solace for the parts of me that ached.

Freeing one of his shirt buttons from its hole, I slipped my fingers inside and rubbed their backs against the soft hair of his chest. Then I freed a second button and slid my whole hand inside. This time, I moved my palm over his nipple. When I felt its sharp rise, I substituted the pad of my thumb for my palm.

He bit my lower lip sharply, then soothed the bruise by sucking it into his mouth, but if he'd meant the injury as a warning, I ignored it. In fact, the tiny pain heightened my pleasure. I wasn't sure if that made me perverted, and I didn't care. The only thing I cared about was pushing the pleasure as far as it would go so that I could reach the pot at the end of the rainbow.

I wasn't going to reach it with a kiss. I knew it, Peter knew it, and the cabbie knew it.

"Almost there, folks," he called back with a trace of dry humor.

I gave a soft, choked cry of frustration and sat back against the seat. Not about to stand for that, Peter drew me to his side and held me tightly. I could feel the tremors that shook his large frame, could see the way he shifted against the bulge in his pants, but the fact that he was as uncomfortable as I was didn't ease my ache. I tried tipping my head and opening my mouth on his neck, but the male tang of his skin and its faint roughness under my tongue only tightened the knot in my belly. I tried shifting position, sliding one of my legs between Peter's, but he wouldn't help me enough to give me the right leverage.

This time he closed his teeth on my ear, but instead of sucking to soothe, he whispered, "Hold on, babe. We'll be there soon."

"I'm on fire," I whispered back.

"Me, too. Soon. Soon."

"I can't wait," I cried softly. That was when I felt him slip a hand between my legs. It climbed the length of my stockings and spread over the warm, soft skin of my thigh before fitting itself to the hot delta that craved it.

A tiny animal sound slipped from my throat, followed by a long, broken breath that grew even more ragged when he began to stroke me. His fingers were on silk; his thumb slipped beneath. Then he seemed to lose patience, because with a single sharp pull he released all four of the small snaps at my crotch.

His fingers found me, touched me. I heard him moan against my temple, and in the wake of the moan came sweet, low, sexy words of praise. I wanted to tell him that I needed more, but I'd momentarily lost the capacity for speech. All I could do was to shift my thighs to offer more of myself to him.

That was when the cab came to a jarring halt at the hotel.

"You owe me four-eighty," the cabbie called.

I nearly screamed in frustration. I would have paid him ten times that amount to keep on driving, but that would have been short-sighted of me. We'd reached a haven. Privacy awaited. While Peter paid the cabbie, I dug my room card from my purse. Peter took it from me as he helped me from the cab, and, hand in hand, we all but ran into the lobby.

The elevator took forever to arrive. Impatiently we waited with our teeth clenched, our hands tightly locked and our heads tipped back to monitor the car's progress. Years before, I'd waited nearly as impatiently for an elevator, only that time my father had been the man with me, and I'd been dancing from foot to foot.

I had no intention of entering the bathroom this time, unless Peter wanted to make love in the tub. I was game for that. I was game for most anything, so desperate was I to feel him inside me.

The elevator arrived. We stepped inside and pressed the proper button, but just as we were turning to each other, two young boys skidded breathlessly into the car. I told myself that that was just fine, that a public elevator was no place for hanky panky, that I'd just stand quietly strangling Peter's fingers with mine until we reached my floor.

But I'd have happily zapped both boys with a real version of the space guns they held, and when I was through doing that, I'd have happily zapped their parents.

The boys raced off at the fourteenth floor and were instantly forgotten. Peter wove a handful of fingers into my hair, leaving his thumb to caress my mouth. My lips parted under their gentle pressure, but only to allow that caress to spread inside. He didn't kiss me, and I didn't miss it, because his eyes, holding mine in their thrall, were silently telling me of all the things he intended to do once we were alone and undressed.

A frisson of excitement shook my limbs, adding to

the quivering inside that I couldn't control. It didn't help that beneath my very lovely navy silk suit, my very lovely white teddy was wide open. That was but one of the things Peter was saying with his electric green eyes.

We nearly missed my floor. The elevator opened, waited, then began to slide shut before Peter bolted forward and put a shoulder to the door. He drew me out with his other hand and didn't let go as we hurried down the hall.

It took him a minute to fit the entry card into the slot. I could hear the frustration in his impatient growl. The door finally opened. We went inside. It closed. We were alone at last.

The silence in the room was broken only by the muted sounds of the city far below and the beat of our thunderous hearts. We didn't waste time listening to the message in the beat. We already knew it. There was no time to lose.

Our coats were no sooner gone when we came together, Peter pulling me so hard and high against him that my feet left the floor. Our mouths fused in a wet, tongue-tangling kiss. I began to push at his suit jacket, then went at it more efficiently when he returned me to the floor. Breathing hard, he ignored my jacket and went straight for my blouse. But his fingers caught on the small pearl buttons, and, while I tugged at his tie, he rasped, "You do it, Jill. I'll tear it." He abandoned my blouse and displaced my hands from his tie, which he proceeded to tear at irreverently.

Hastily I dispensed with my jacket. Taking shallow little breaths, I kicked my shoes aside, unzipped my skirt and pushed it down my legs, then hopped from one foot to the other until I was free. Heedless of the fine fabric, I tossed it blindly aside. My fingers raced to my blouse, but there I paused, because that was what Peter had done. His tie and shirt were gone, his belt unfastened and his trousers unzipped, but he was staring at me, at that part of me between my waist and my knees that was so erotically displayed.

I didn't give a damn about erotic displays, at least not about mine. I wanted to see Peter. I wanted to touch him, taste him, satisfy the awful craving that was eating me alive. So I covered the small distance between us, opened my mouth on his chest and I slid my hands, palms flat, into his trousers.

He was hot and heavy, fully-aroused and throbbing with desire. My fingers closed around him. I strained upward in an attempt to align our body parts.

Peter wasn't having that just yet. Capturing my mouth in a suctioning swoop, he forced his hands between us, fiddled with the buttons of my blouse for another impatient second, then tugged. The pearls didn't make a sound as they fell to the carpet, not that we'd have heard if they had. We were too busy trying to kiss, trying to breathe, trying to get me out of my blouse and Peter out of his pants.

Buck naked, he was a strong and beautiful animal. I only had a second to register that fact when he slipped one arm around my back and the other under my bottom and lifted me against him. His mouth met mine. I coiled both arms around his neck, overlapping them tightly. My legs wound around his waist.

In a single fluid movement, he turned, lowered me

to the turned-back bed and thrust deep into me. The shock of it brought a sharp cry from my throat.

He went very still. "Jill?"

I panted softly and tightened my arms around his neck.

"I've hurt you."

"Oh, no." My body had already begun to adjust to his size, and even at that very first moment of possession, my reaction was more one of surprise than pain. As we lay coupled so tightly, I could feel tendrils of pleasure blotting out surprise, and at the tips of those tendrils were tiny pinpoints of heat.

A fine sheen of sweat broke out over my skin. I closed my eyes. The thought that Peter was embedded inside me was nearly as electric as his eyes.

In a gentle move, as though he were gauging my ability to take him, he carefully undulated his hips. But if he'd intended it as an exploratory measure, it was his undoing. "I can't stop," he breathed hoarsely, then more frantically, "I can't stop, Jill." His broad shoulders trembled under the force of restraint as, devoid of gentleness, he reared up over me.

He drew back, then slammed forward. I cried out again, this time at the fire his thrust stoked, and when he drew back again, I matched his motion.

There was no stopping either of us, then. His body grew slick with sweat. His hair fell in swaying spikes on his forehead as he drove into me again and again. I met each thrust head-on, raised my legs on his back to deepen his penetration. I couldn't seem to get enough of him, nor could he of me. Sliding a hand under me, he lifted my bottom and drove even higher.

I think he'd have possessed my entire body if he'd been able—not that what he was doing was much different. The point of his possession seemed to control everything else about me, from the way my fingernails raked his damp back, to the way my head thrashed from side to side, to the short, sharp bits of breath I labored to take.

In a soul-shattering moment, I sucked in a lungful of air and arched into a powerful climax. The spasms went on and on. They were enhanced by Peter's explosive movements, then his final grunting plunge. As his big body shook, I felt the surge of liquid heat deep inside.

For what seemed an eternity, he lay over me, but I didn't mind the weight. It was warm, male, delicious, as was the scent that hovered around us. Eyes closed, I savored that, like an after-dinner drink taken on the tails of a fine red wine.

When he started to move, I clenched my legs tight around him. "Don't go," I whispered, suddenly afraid that he'd up and leave. I might have climaxed, but I was far from sated.

Taking me with him, he rolled to his side. I looked up into his face to find his green eyes heavily lidded and warm. "I'm not going anywhere," he said hoarsely. Levering himself up on an elbow, he closed his hand around my leg, which was under him, and gently pulled it forward. "I don't want to crush it." He eased it down next to the other. His expression was almost reverent as he watched his own fingers skim the silk-clad length.

I looked down then to see what he had, but I saw

nothing reverent in a pair of legs sheathed in sheer navy, a pure white garter belt and a white teddy whose lacy hem was bunched up under my breasts.

Peter was looking there, too. He ran his fingertips under my breasts. "You are beautiful," he whispered.

"I think wanton is the word," I whispered back. Though there was no one to hear us, it was an intimate moment.

He fanned his hand over my stomach. "Wanton matched the way I felt. I don't know how I made it through your show." He grunted. "I don't know how I made it through the past few weeks."

I sank a hand into his hair and tugged. "You didn't call me."

"You didn't call me."

"You're the man. You're supposed to do it."

"These are the eighties. You're an independent woman."

"Not that independent."

"How was I to know? You women have us so confused sometimes we don't know whether we're coming or going."

His reference to women in the plural was a generic one, which was the way I took it. I wasn't about to consider the other women he'd known personally, not at a moment when he was all mine.

But he felt it important. Sobering, he shaped his hand to my jaw and said, "I may have been pretty wild as a kid, but lately there haven't been a whole lot of different women in my life." His thumb coasted over my skin. "I'm clean. You won't catch anything from me, but I haven't guarded you against pregnancy. You're not using anything, are you?''

I shook my head. ''I bought condoms.'' My cheeks went red. ''They're in my purse.''

''That's good. I wouldn't want a pregnant purse on my hands.'' His thumb moved higher to explore my flushed skin. ''Are you embarrassed because you left them in your purse, or because you bought them in the first place?''

''Both. I've never done anything like this before.''

''What kind of risk did we take?''

''Not a big one. It's the wrong time of the month. Besides, I don't get pregnant easily.'' His eyes requested an elaboration that I felt it only fair to give. ''I didn't use anything for three years, and nothing happened.''

''You wanted children then?''

I nodded, but I refused to dwell on what might have been. I refused to dwell on anything that might take away from the moment and Peter. Knowing the perfect diversion, I dropped my gaze to his toes and slowly drew my eyes north. I'd seen his upper half before, but the lower half was new and exciting. His legs were long, lean and scarred, but beautiful nonetheless and spattered with the same dark hair that painted patterns over his chest. His thighs were tightly muscled. His sex, at rest now, lay in a thick nest of hair.

Suddenly he shifted, rising to his knees.

''Where are you going?'' I asked in alarm.

''Nowhere.'' He took one of my legs, put my foot flat against his belly and ran his hands up the slender length of dark blue silk. When he reached my garter belt, he unfastened its hook, released the stocking from its hold and slowly rolled it down.

I was fascinated. When I'd bought the lingerie, it had been with the wearing in mind. I'd been feeling sexy and wanted to feel even sexier. On some level, I must have wanted Peter to see it and think it as sexy as I did, but through all my fantasies I never pictured him removing it.

Maybe that was why I found it so exciting. Watching him so intent on his task, though his skin barely touched mine, I felt my heart begin to pound.

When he finished with the first stocking and dropped it to the floor, he gently shifted that leg aside and took up the other one. He repeated the unsheathing process, revealing more and more pale skin. Again, when my leg was bare, he dropped the stocking to the floor. This time, keeping my foot flat against his middle, he bent my knee out and ran his hand all along the inside of my leg.

With one leg on the other side of him and my knee as he'd bent it, I was completely exposed to his gaze. I found that, too, exciting. He made me proud of my body, proud to be a woman. When, of their own accord, my breasts began to swell with that pride, Peter looked their way. His gaze rose higher to my face, fell back to my breasts, then lowered to the most private of my feminine parts.

His thumb touched me, then his fingers. He opened me, stroked me, teased my secret flesh until it was hot and moist. By this time I'd turned my head against the intensity of the pleasure. When he suddenly slid his hands under me and up my back, then lifted me to face him, I opened my eyes.

"Hold on," he instructed in a whisper as he draped my arms around his neck.

For a minute we sat there, locked eye to eye. I knew the story my face told. My eyes were bright, my cheeks pink, my lips moist, parted and inviting.

Peter's face held tell-tale signs of its own. His skin was damp, his eyes intense. Small brackets on either side of his nose told of the self-control he was exerting. And his mouth was open to allow the free passage of what was very close to heavy breathing.

Looping my arms loosely around his neck, I held on. I watched him, watched him closely.

Reaching behind me, he unhooked my garter belt. It fell aside to leave me totally bare from the waist down. Peter looked at my stomach, looked at his hands on my stomach, looked at the gentle movement of my flesh when he began to lightly knead it. His fingers slipped lower, seeming irrevocably drawn to the pale nest between my legs. But at the first small gasp I gave when he drew me open, he moved his hands higher again. They didn't stop this time until they cupped my breasts.

With a care that was in sharp contrast to the frenzied way we'd made love earlier, he took hold of the bunched hem of the teddy and drew it over my head. I had to release his neck to free my arms, and before I could grab onto him again, he threaded his fingers through mine and held my hands off to the sides.

For the first time, I felt shy. I wasn't sure whether it was my total nudity, or the shameless way I was sitting, or the intentness with which Peter studied my body, but at that moment I would have given anything for a sheet to draw up.

"Don't look away," Peter whispered just as I realized that I had. "You are—" he paused, as though seeking the words "—the realization of a fantasy. I've been thinking about just this, imagining it since the first time I saw you." Placing my hands at the back of his waist, he drew me onto his lap. As my body came into full contact with his, I forgot my shyness. For one thing, he was magnificently aroused and made no attempt to hide it. For another, the sense of homecoming was stunning.

We fit perfectly. My head found its niche on his shoulder, my breasts nestled gently against his chest, my thighs framed his hips. I felt comfortable and content. I felt protected. I felt whole.

Which wasn't to say that I complained when Peter tipped his head to nibble on my neck. Or that I fretted when he began to play with my breasts. Or that I raised a fuss when the magic of his fingers stirred up new yearnings between my legs.

This time there was tenderness. We explored each other more slowly, savoring all the little things we'd missed in the savagery of our first joining. But where I'd thought nothing could match the explosiveness of that first time, I was wrong. The slow rise, the gentle savoring, the feint and parry, the holding back—all led to a wildness that was every bit as combustive as savagery.

This time when we lay in the aftermath of orgasm, our limp bodies slick with sweat, our hearts pounding against each other, I couldn't deny the fact that Peter did to me what no man had ever done. I'd thought it earlier, now I thought it again. He made me feel whole.

Peter took it one step further. When he'd recovered enough to speak, he raised himself on an elbow above me, pressed a gentle kiss to my lips and said, "I love you."

I hadn't expected that. I didn't want it. The words were too strong, too soon. They suggested and demanded. They evoked thoughts of things I wasn't ready to face.

He must have seen the panic in my eyes, because he ran his tongue over my chin, ending in a feather-light kiss, and said, "I'm not asking you to love me back. Not yet. All I want is time together to see if it's real. There's been something between us from the start. Part of it's physical, and that physical thing builds when we're apart, so we come together and think of nothing but sex."

Cupping my throat, he looked me straight in the eye. "But there's more, Jill. There's a whole lot more. I know you don't want it to be there, but it is—just like when we first met, you didn't want there to be anything physical, but you reached a point where you couldn't deny it. You'll reach that point about the rest. I know you will. But we need time together for that."

I didn't want to think about love. I *couldn't* think about love. Neither, though, could I think about walking away from Peter. I'd come to New York to see him. I wanted to be with him. If he wanted to think about deeper things, that was fine, as long as I could just enjoy him in the here-and-now.

"Time, Jill," he repeated, pinning me with a pale green stare. "Can you give me that?"

"On one condition," I whispered. "You'll have to feed me. I'm starved."

8

Swansy was in an uproar when I reached her house early Wednesday morning. She was watching the talk show that she watched every morning at that time, and the topic was rape. "Have you ever heard anythin' so stupid?" she warbled, then snorted. "Men bein' raped by women—it can't happen unless the man wants it, and then it ain't no rape. But those men yammer on, tryin' to drum up sympathy for the pain they've suffered. I don't buy it. Don't buy it for a minute."

I studied the three men alternately captured on the television screen. "They seem sincere enough," I said. "Apparently they buy their story, even if you don't."

"It's hogwash. Men are bigger 'n stronger 'n we are. They have the advantage every time, so we have to be on our toes up here—" she tapped her head "—if we don't want 'em to run roughshod over us."

I looked at Swansy, so petite, yet so strong, and though I wasn't making any judgments about the possibility of a man being raped, I couldn't argue the merit of a woman's being on her toes. I'd gone flatfooted through the past four days, taking everything

Peter had given. Now I needed to get back on the ball.

Rebecca nudged her cold nose under my hand. I was stroking her muzzle when Swansy said, "Well?"

"Well, what?" I wasn't really in the frame of mind to discuss men who'd been raped.

She came through for me as she had so many times before. Pressing the remote control, she turned off the TV. "Sit down and tell me, girl. Tell me everything."

I sat. Rebecca put her head on my thigh. "Where should I begin?"

Swansy's smile was sweet and knowing. "How was the flight?"

"Smooth."

"The hotel?"

"Lovely."

"The show?"

"Wonderful."

"Did they love you?"

I shrugged and gave a sheepish smile. Though she couldn't see it, I like to think it came out in my voice. "I guess so. We sold lots."

"And your man?"

"My man?"

She didn't speak, just sat there directing that sweet, expectant smile my way.

"Peter," I said. I dragged in a deep breath, held it for a minute, then let it slip back out through my teeth. "Peter was incredible."

Swansy's smile didn't widen. She wasn't about to let me know whether my comment pleased her or not. For a blind person, she played poker like a pro.

And like a sap, I fell for her bluff and began to talk. But then, that was what I'd come for. Swansy was my sounding board. My thoughts desperately needed an airing.

"He came to the reception on Friday night, and except for a meeting he had with a client on Sunday morning and Monday night when I went home, we were together every minute. He is a...remarkable man."

I wasn't sure how else to describe him. An extraordinary lover? A great lay? A sexual wizard? I didn't really want to tell Swansy that Peter and I had spent the better part of our time together in bed, because I was afraid she'd get the wrong idea.

Then again, it wasn't the wrong idea. It was exactly what we'd done. But what Peter had taught me about lust would burn Swansy's ears.

Then again, maybe not.

But where a man and a woman were concerned, some things were sacred.

So I focused on what we'd done *out* of bed. "We spent a lot of time at the gallery. I felt I owed it to Moni, and to Bill and Celia. And when Peter had to work, I sat in a corner of his office pretending to be a law student observing. But otherwise we were free. He took me to his favorite French restaurant. We ferried out to the Statue of Liberty. We went to the Museum of Modern Art. We saw a movie at midnight, then ate huge corned beef sandwiches at an all-night deli. And we walked up and down the avenues, just talking."

"Sounds nice," Swansy said.

"It was. I've always hated New York, but I think that's because I've let it use me, rather than the other way around. Peter and I used it for the things it had to offer. But there are times, like when we were talking over coffee, when we could have been anywhere. The city took a back seat then."

Swansy nodded.

I sank deeper into the chair, my thoughts distant as I absently scratched Rebecca's head. "We talked about everything. That surprised me."

"How come?"

"Because we're so different. We come at life from very different angles. I originally came from money. He didn't. He's living with it now. I'm not. We have contrasting views on some things, but still we were able to talk. I can see why he's a success as a lawyer. He's bright and quick and so logical that it's sometimes hard to disagree with him."

"But you did."

"Sure, I did. He liked that. It makes me wonder about the other women he's known. I can't believe he's been attracted to 'yes' ladies all these years."

"He never married any of 'em. Maybe that's why. Maybe what he had with 'em was sex."

That's what he has with me, I almost said, but Peter swore it wasn't so. More than once over the three days we spent together, he told me he loved me, and never did he do it in the throes of passion. He pointed that out quite bluntly. It was early on Tuesday afternoon, when I was getting my things together to check out of the hotel. Peter took me standing up, with my back to the fire escape instructions tacked on the door. We were both fully clothed—and as hot as ever.

"I'll miss you," he murmured when it was over.

"Don't kid me, bud," I teased. "It's my body you'll miss. It's been a slave to yours since Friday night."

He didn't crack a smile. "No. I'll miss you. All of you. That's what I love." He planted a wet kiss on the pulse point on my neck. "If I only loved your body, I'd tell your body I loved it, but do I? Have I ever said those words when we were making love?"

I hadn't thought about it before, but when I did, I had to admit that he hadn't. I shook my head.

"That's because my love for you isn't rooted in my balls. It's here—" he touched his heart "—and here—" he touched his head. "If love is worth beans, it's rational. It involves things like respect and trust. Very rational."

I'd felt threatened by the words when he'd said them, and I still did. Maybe it had something to do with what Swansy had said about a woman having to use her brains to fight a man's brawn. What was a woman to do when a man used both brains *and* brawn?

"Well," I sighed, returning to Swansy and the present, "whatever it was with his other woman, it isn't now. He's not seeing anyone special."

"'Cept you." Her voice held a very subtle note of inquiry.

I was quiet for a time before acknowledging it. "Except me. He's flying up this weekend."

After a pregnant pause, she said, "You don't sound real happy about that."

"I'm not sure if I am."

With the nudge of her foot, she began to rock back and forth, but she didn't say a word.

So I went ahead and voiced the worries that had been nagging at me since I'd left New York the day before. "I was happy at the time. We'd had such a fun time together, Peter and I, that I didn't want to leave him. When he suggested he come up this weekend, I jumped at the idea." I looked at my hands, straightened my fingers, stacked one set on the other. "Then I headed back here, and the closer I got, the more confused I felt." I looked at Swansy. "I don't know what to make of our relationship. I don't know what I want it to be."

"What does Peter want?"

"Everything."

"Everything?"

"Everything—well, maybe that's not true. Or I don't know if it's true. We haven't talked about the future. I don't know what he wants down the road, but he says he loves me. He says it's the real thing, and that it's going to grow. He says that I'm everything he's dreamed about for years."

Swansy sighed voluminously. "Ah. So pretty. He'd sure make a better script writer than the loony who writes—"

"I'm serious, Swansy!" I cried. "Peter can be straight-forward and tough and demanding, but he's a romantic. He says beautiful things to me, and they're all from the heart. How can I deal with that?"

"Do you love him?"

"Of course not. I loved Adam. I won't love another man. And besides, I haven't known Peter long enough. He hasn't known *me* long enough. Two extended weekends—that's all we've had. How can he say he loves me after just that?"

Swansy rocked, and smiled.

"How can he, Swansy? Isn't this whole thing a little fanciful?"

"If it's fanciful, that's because you need it to be. He'd be good for you, Jillie."

"Good? He'd be awful! Look at him. He's a hotshot lawyer. He buzzes in and out of courtrooms all over the Northeast, and when he's not traveling on business, he's doing bizarre things like exploring uninhabited islands in the South Seas."

"Sounds exciting."

"Maybe to you, but I like my life here. I like the quiet and the routine. I like the sameness of it."

"You feel comfortable here."

"Yes!"

"Secure."

"Yes!"

"You feel completely satisfied, a total woman."

I took a breath and opened my mouth, then shut it without saying a thing. I should have known Swansy would cut right to the heart of the matter.

"What am I going to do?" I wailed softly.

"What do you want to do?"

"Turn back the clock and make things the way they were before."

"Would you feel like a total woman then?"

"I was happy then."

"You didn't know what you were missing."

"I knew what I was missing. I just didn't want it."

But she was shaking her head. "You didn't know. You hadn't met him then. Sorry, girl. Even if you could turn back the clock, you're a different woman now. Nothin's ever goin' to be the same."

I stared at her hard, hoping she could feel it. "What kind of friend are you? I came here for comfort."

Back and forth she rocked. "You came here for me to tell you that what you did with that man in New York was all right, and I'm sayin' it was."

"That's just *it*. It *was* all right in New York. I was a different person there. But now he's coming here, and I'm not sure I'll be able to handle it."

"You will."

"I won't. This is Adam's turf."

"Hogwash!" Swansy muttered, suddenly impatient. She stopped rocking, and without the creak of the runners on the floor, the room seemed starkly quiet, a perfect foil for her high, wavering voice. "It was always more your turf than Adam's. Face it, girl. Right from the start, you were the one who fit in here, not Adam."

"But this was where he lived. This was where *we* lived. This town, that little house on the bluff are all part of my life with Adam."

Swansy sighed. "Know somethin', girl?"

"No. What?"

"If Adam hadn't died, you'd never have stayed together."

"Swansy!"

"It's true. So you can set this place up in your mind as a shrine, but if he was alive, he'd have left."

"But...but he loved me," I argued in a small voice.

"I'm sure he did, but he wasn't as strong as you. He'd've stuck with the fishin' as long as he could, then he'd've made you choose between this place and him. I'm guessin' you'd've chosen this place, so don't talk about it being Adam's turf."

I was feeling a little defeated. "You know what I mean."

"No, I don't. I see that y've lived here alone for double the time you lived here with Adam. I see that y're on the other side of thirty and still sleepin' in an empty bed. And I see that if you keep on the way y'are, y'll find yourself an old lady like me with no one to leave her house to when she dies."

I glared at her, then grumbled, "You see an awful lot, for a blind lady."

"When the Good Lord took my sight, He gave me something in its stead."

"Yeah. A sharp tongue."

"Better a sharp tongue than a deaf ear. I ain't got no deaf ear. I hear what you're saying, and what you're not saying, and if you're coming to me for advice, then that's what I'm givin' you."

"I don't like it."

"So what're you going to do?"

"Change the subject."

"Fine," she bit out, then went quiet. After a full minute she resumed her rocking. Her expression, which had been as cross as her voice moments before, slowly gentled to the one I knew and loved.

Nothing had been settled. I felt as confused as I'd been when I arrived. Somewhere deep inside, I knew that Swansy wasn't all wrong, but I couldn't quite separate the right part from the wrong part, and the whole thing was getting me down. I needed a diversion.

"Swansy, about this business with Cooper," I began, testing the waters to see if she'd go along with the change. I took her silence as a positive sign. "I've been thinking."

"Don't know when you've had time to do that," she murmured to herself—wholly for my benefit. I figured she couldn't quite let me get away scot-free, but it could have been worse.

"I've been thinking," I repeated, gaining courage as I turned my mind in the direction of those thoughts. "Something isn't quite right."

"Course not. Cooper's in trouble."

"I know that, and I know that Peter is doing everything he can possibly do on the legal end. Still, something isn't quite right."

Swansy rocked.

"On this end," I added.

Swansy rocked.

"I've been thinking. Someone has to know something he's not telling us. I can't believe that a total stranger waltzed onto the *Free Reign*, went straight to Cooper's cabin, straight to the laundry bag with his name on it and stashed stolen diamonds there, then waltzed back off the boat without anyone knowing a thing about it. Cooper never leaves the boat unattended. Someone was there the whole time. All along, we've contended that the person on guard was asleep when whoever it was stashed the diamonds. I keep wondering about that.''

Swansy continued rocking, encouraging me on with a soft, ''Um-hmm.''

''The guard is assigned on a rotating basis, so theoretically any one of the crew members could have been on duty when the diamonds were stashed. Peter and I talked with each of them. Except for Benjie.''

I watched her closely, but she gave nothing away. So I went a step further. ''Those men are all hardworking guys. When they finally agree to talk, they're blunt, heart-on-their-sleeve fellows. Neither Peter nor I had cause to doubt any of them. But we weren't able to talk with Benjie.''

The creak of the rocker came and went, came and went.

''Benjie is the only member of that crew who has the slightest blemish on his record.'' I threw an arm to the top of my head and looked toward the ceiling. ''I mean, I know it's absurd even to be thinking this, because he's only twenty, and he's strictly a two-bit troublemaker, and I can't imagine how he'd possibly have connected with anyone big enough to be involved in smuggling diamonds into the country—'' Grabbing a breath, I looked back at Swansy. ''But, damn it, Benjie is so *hostile*. I think he knows something.''

My words hung in the air for a good long time before breaking apart like so many pieces of dried

mud. I waited for Swansy to pick up the gauntlet in
Benjie's defense. After all, she'd known him far
longer than I. She remembered when he'd been born.

But she didn't pick up the gauntlet. Instead, she
said, "Could be."

I grew instantly alert. "Could be?" I repeated expectantly.

She rocked silently.

"Lord, Swansy, don't stop there. You know something, don't you?" When she didn't answer, I said,
"This is Cooper's future we're talking about. The
trial won't be happening for a good three months, and
in the meanwhile he's going through hell. We both
know that he's innocent, but if you know something
else—"

"I don't *know* something. But there are certain possibilities."

"Like Benjie being involved in the smuggling.
Why would he have done it? Who would he have
done it for? And how could he stand around here and
keep his mouth shut when his own brother is taking
the flak?"

As Swansy rocked, she pursed her lips. I schooled
myself to remain silent. After all, if she could pull a
Swansy on me, I could pull one right back on her.

It worked. After a time, she said, "Nothin' was
ever simple when it came to Benjie. There's a whole
lot goin' on in his mind. Maybe he has a right to it.
I don't know. An' maybe he has a right to take it out
on Cooper. I don't know that, either. But I wouldn't
be surprised if he knows more than he's lettin' on."

"I'm going to talk with him," I said and started to rise from the chair.

"Stay put," Swansy ordered. She waited until she heard the rustle of the cushions before sitting forward in her rocker and reaching for my hand. "Think first, Jillie. Don't do anythin' rash. I may be all wrong, and if that's so, you're only gonna stir up hard feelings."

She had a point. But I couldn't sit and do nothing. Besides, I was a fast thinker. "Okay," I said. "I've thought. And what I'm going to do, very calmly, is to talk with Cooper. He's protective of Benjie, so I won't make any accusations, but a few subtle questions might do it. I want to know whether Cooper has any suspicions of his own."

Giving my hand a squeeze, Swansy sat back in her chair and resumed rocking.

No one was home at Cooper's house. I busied myself visiting people in town until noon, when he returned. He wanted to know first thing about my trip, so I gave him a rundown on the show. Then he asked about the night I'd spent with my family.

"They're the same," I said lightly. "They always will be. Dad and Ian are like two peas in a pod. They see life in terms of dollar signs. Samantha is the social climber. My mother is the political power broker. Dinners at the Madigan house are high-pressure affairs."

Cooper watched me closely with those dark eyes of his. "You seem pretty calm. It didn't throw you so much this time?"

"No. Maybe I'm finally getting stronger."

"Maybe you had other things on your mind."

"Maybe." I wasn't sure how much of that I wanted to broach with Cooper.

I was trying to decide, when he said, "Peter called before I left this morning. He mentioned that he'd spent time with you."

"He did?"

Cooper nodded slowly.

I moved to fill what promised to be an awkward silence. "I watched him work. He has associates running here and there doing research and preparing motions while he focuses on the creative end. It's very impressive. I wish you could have been there."

"No, you don't."

The look on his face told me I wasn't going to get away with much. "You're right. It would have been embarrassing, what with us making love on top of the desk." I took a quick breath, then raced on. "Cooper, we have to talk about Benjie."

Cooper's mouth twitched at the corners. "Did you really do it on a desk?"

I made a face. "Of course not." Then, serious again, I repeated, "*Benjie*, Cooper. Is anything special going on with him?"

"But you did make it together?"

I sighed. "Do I ask what you do with your women?"

"No. But this is different. Peter is the first man I've met in a long time who's strong enough for you."

I looked him straight in those opaque eyes of his. "I want to talk about Benjie."

He eyed me right back. "I don't."

"Why not?"

"Because there's no need. Benjie is my concern. No one else's."

I'd already blown my chances for subtlety, so I went right to the heart of the matter. "I think he's hiding something. I think he knows more about those diamonds then he's letting on."

Cooper's eyes narrowed slightly. "What makes you think that?"

"He's been so surly lately. He resents my presence, and Peter's presence. I think he's afraid we'll uncover something he doesn't want uncovered."

"Like what?"

"Like...*I* don't know. Like maybe he saw someone board the boat and stash the diamonds. Like maybe he knew the person. Like maybe he was doing someone else's bidding and stashed them there himself." I tossed a hand in the air. "It's bizarre to be thinking that a twenty-year-old could have done that, especially when he's your brother, but something's strange about this whole thing, Cooper."

I paused. Cooper's feelings were totally shuttered behind his dark eyes, but the darkness itself made me uneasy. It was thicker than usual.

I sighed. "Do you know anything? Has Benjie said anything to you? I know that you've always tried to protect him, but if he's somehow involved in this and you don't speak up, you'll be the one to take the fall."

Cooper stretched his long legs in front of him, but

there was nothing easygoing in his lines. "I want
Benjie left out of this."

"You do know something."

"Benjie is innocent."

"But he's somehow involved. Tell me, Cooper.
Please. I don't want you going to prison for something you didn't do."

"You hired Peter so that wouldn't happen."

"But he can only do so much."

Cooper stared off at the wall. His expression was
tighter than ever when he looked back at me. "You're
spending a lot of money on this, Jill, even though you
know I didn't want it. Well, I've agreed to be represented by your man, but that doesn't mean that I've
sold him my soul. You're right; he can only do so
much. I'm not asking that he prove me innocent, or
that he prove anyone else guilty. All I'm asking is
that he establish reasonable doubt in the minds of
those jurors."

"But if Benjie has information that can prove your
innocence...."

"Leave Benjie alone."

"He's an adult. At some point he has to take responsibility for his actions."

"Do you think I don't know that?" Cooper barked.

I backed off a bit, but only to the extent of mod-
erating my voice to a more gentle tone. "Then tell
me what you know. Tell *Peter* what you know. If
Benjie saw something, he'll be protected. If he was
actually involved, he could get immunity by testifying
for the state."

"Leave it, Jill." His voice was as darkly ominous and unyielding as his eyes.

I felt pushed to a crossroads, where I had to choose between respecting Cooper's wishes for the sake of our friendship or risking that friendship for the sake of his future. It was a no-win situation.

"I don't like this," I whispered, my voice breaking.

"Don't you dare cry."

"I don't like it at all."

Leaning forward, he reached for my hand. When I offered it, he closed his fingers tightly around it. "Everything's going to be okay, Jill. Trust me. Trust Peter. I'll be fine."

How many times I said those words in the course of the next few days I didn't know, but at some point they ceased referring to Cooper and began referring to me. That point came when I realized I missed Peter.

I didn't know why I missed him. On top of my worry about Cooper, I had plenty to do to catch up on what I'd missed while I'd been gone. But still there were those times—odd times, quiet times—when I felt lonely in ways I hadn't felt since right after Adam had died.

It was bad enough that I still craved him. I'd have thought that after the sexually active four days we'd spent together, my body would be sated. The problem was that sexually active wasn't necessarily sexually exhausted. All I had to do was to recall any one of the things we'd done together and my temperature rose.

Worse, though, the craving wasn't only physical. I kept thinking about the time we'd spent together in New York and how much I'd enjoyed it. I remembered the satisfaction I felt when we talked, even when we disagreed. I remembered the meals we'd eaten together. I remembered showering while he shaved. I remembered the silences we'd shared, when we'd each been lost in our own thoughts with only the link of our arms or our hands to connect us. I remembered the pleasure in that, and I missed it.

I'll be fine, I told myself. It was the novelty of Peter that had gotten to me. I'd calm down. I'd get used to being alone again. I'd fall back into the old groove. That's what I wanted.

Still, I looked forward to his arrival with growing enthusiasm, and by the time Saturday finally arrived, I felt as though I'd been waiting four weeks, rather than four days to see him.

I drove into Bangor to meet his plane, and the feeling was much like the one I'd had the week before, when I'd first caught sight of him at the show. At the moment he passed through the terminal door, I felt everything else in the room fall into a hazy background. This time, there was nothing to shatter the moment. I went toward him, first at a properly sedate walk, then a bit faster, finally at a light run. Peter had set his carryon down by the time I reached him, and when I flew into his arms, he caught me tight, whipped me off my feet and whirled me around.

We kissed long and well.

"Let's get out of here," he growled at last. With his bag over his shoulder and his coat over his arm to hide his arousal from the world, he ushered me to the parking lot.

We talked the entire time during the drive to my house—about his work, about Cooper and Benjie, about little nothings from the weekend before. As soon as Peter stopped for a breath, I picked up, and the instant I stopped, Peter started again. Listening to us, one would have thought that we either had to squeeze a whole lot in a very little time, or that we were totally starved for conversation.

I'm not sure it was conversation that we were starved for. As soon as we parked the car and went inside, Peter dropped his things and picked me up in his arms.

"Where'll it be?" he asked in a hoarse whisper.

But the light in his eyes asked another question, one I'd been asking myself since I'd returned. It was one thing for Peter and I to make love in the neutral territory of a hotel in New York, another for us to make love in my house. I'd never doubted that we would make love if he came. But where? In my room or his? Which bed would we share during the night— the one he'd slept in before, or the one I'd shared with Adam?

When I'd first returned from New York, I'd have said his room. Just as I'd chosen the Park Lane over his Central Park South apartment. Both involved less of a commitment. But in the course of the past three days, I'd done a turnaround. I couldn't tell Peter I loved him, but I could tell him how much he'd come to mean to me.

"My room," I whispered, and he took me straight there. Laying me down on the bed, he came down on top of me. After kissing me senseless, he rolled away long enough to tug off my jeans and release himself from his pants. Then he slid into me with all the ease and excitement of a cherished lover.

He drove everything else from my mind. Not once did I think of Adam, of the fact that this had been our bed or that I'd sworn I'd never share it with another man. There was a certain rightness in what Peter and I were doing. Between that rightness and the mind-blowing rapture that burst upon and between us, there was no room for doubt.

Nor did I doubt myself when, much later, having properly undressed and made love a second, more leisurely time, we lay quietly in each other's arms. Peter's presence had settled into my bedroom, taking it over, leaving no room for anyone else. I was feeling too content for second thoughts.

I had second thoughts about Cooper, though. I discussed them in greater detail with Peter, and when we stopped in to see Swansy later that afternoon, we raised them with her.

"Cooper wants Benjie left alone," I said, "and he's rigid enough about it that I know something's up. What is it, Swansy? Do you know?"

Swansy shook her head.

Peter tried his hand. "I've spent a lot of time on this case. Things are looking pretty good, since the government can't offer either a motive or a connection between Cooper and any known smugglers—or crooks of any kind, for that matter. Customs officials were tipped off by an anonymous phone call, but they have no idea who made it and who, if not Cooper, it was aimed to catch. So the only evidence against Cooper is the diamonds themselves. With the right approach, I can probably sway the jury. Probably. Not definitely. And if things go against us, Cooper winds up in jail. Anything, Swansy, anything you know would be a help.''

''I don't know anythin' about diamond smugglers,'' Swansy protested, almost as though we'd accused her of being one.

''Then about Cooper and Benjie,'' I prompted. ''Why is Benjie so difficult? And why is Cooper so determined to shield him?''

''B'cause Cooper Drake is a loyal man. You know that, girl.''

''I sure do. But blind loyalty's no good.''

''Tell that to a man in love.''

Peter murmured in my ear, ''She has a point. I can personally vouch for that.'' When I shot him a don't-confuse-the-issues look, he added a quick, ''That's why spouses can't be called to testify against each other in court.''

I rubbed my head against his cheek. ''But Cooper's not in love, and he doesn't have a spouse. He loved a girl a long time ago—''

''Still loves,'' Swansy corrected. ''Name's Cyrill.''

''Cyrill? Was she from here?''

''Nope. Worked here, though. She was a waitress at Sam's when it was run by Sam's daddy.''

"And Cooper loved her."

"Dearly."

Over my shoulder, Peter seemed deep in thought. So I turned back to Swansy. "Blind loyalty? Between Cooper and Cyrill, or Cooper and Benjie?"

Swansy shrugged.

I had the distinct feeling that there was a message in something she'd said, but I wasn't quite sure what it was. "So Cooper's protecting Benjie the way he would have protected Cyrill if she'd still been around?"

Swansy shrugged.

Peter was more on the ball than I. "Cooper's protecting Cyrill now?"

Swansy began to rock in her chair.

I turned to Peter. "Cooper's never mentioned her. Neither has anyone else in town. I had no idea she existed."

"Like Cooper, the people in this town protect their own."

"But Cyrill isn't one of their own."

"Cooper is. So's Benjie."

"But what does any of this have to do with the charges against Cooper?" I cried, looking up at Peter. He looked down at me. Then we both looked over at the little old lady in the chair. "Swansy?"

She rocked, shook her head, closed her eyes.

"Come on, Swansy," Peter coaxed. "We'll find out anyway. You'll save us time by telling us what you know."

Very softly and in a warble that sounded uncharacteristically vulnerable, she said, "I'm one of the townsfolk, and Cooper's one of mine. Don't make me betray him more 'n I already have.''

Her plea hit home. Much as I wanted to help Cooper, I knew that I couldn't ask Swansy another thing. She'd done her share. She'd pointed us in a new direction, and in so doing, she felt she'd betrayed a friend. No, I couldn't ask her for more.

That didn't mean I couldn't ask anyone else. When I looked up at Peter, I saw him thinking the very same thing. I also saw him thinking about the reticence of the townspeople and the risk we took of alienating Cooper.

We had our work cut out for us.

9

Peter and I spent most of Sunday visiting with people we'd discussed the case with the month before. Our excuse was a need to double-check certain statements they'd made, and we threw in mention of Cyrill as casually as possible, but we didn't fool anyone. The standard reaction to the mention of her name was a clamming up. Clearly everyone knew who she was, but no one was talking. That left us to do some detective work on our own.

Her full name was Cyrill Stockland. We got that much after spending Sunday night poring through the cartons of records that sat in the basement of Sam's Saloon. She'd waitressed there for seven months, twenty-two years before. The forwarding address was a diner in a small town in New Hampshire, and though we didn't expect that she'd still be there, we drove over Monday morning just in case.

Peter had already decided to stay with me until Tuesday. I wish I could say that I approached the search for Cyrill with utter gravity, given Cooper's predicament, but the fact was I felt a distinct sense of adventure. Spending time with Peter, traveling through the back roads of New England with him, was a treat.

As far as the New Hampshire diner was concerned, Cyrill Stockland didn't exist. The cook, though, sent us to see the owner of a rooming house where most of the town's transient help stayed at one point or another. The owner remembered Cyrill.

"That one was a beauty," he told us, though only after he'd moved out of earshot of his wife, who, like him, looked to be in her late sixties. "My Mary didn't like her. Stuck up, she said. Had fancy notions, she said." He shrugged his stooped shoulders. "Me, I just thought she was pretty. Had a nice beau, too. Tall fellow. Dark."

I wondered if that was Cooper, but if the man had known more at one time, he'd long since forgotten. He was able, though, to give us the name and address of a country inn in the northwest corner of Massachusetts.

"Used to be run by some friends of mine," he explained. "When she said she wanted to move on, I sent her there." He scratched his sparsely haired head. "Don't know if she ever made it, or if the new owners ever heard of her, but it's worth a try."

We had nothing to lose. Since we'd already driven so far south, it made sense for Peter to rent a car early Tuesday morning and continue on into the city while I drove back home. A country inn sounded like a perfect place to spend Monday night.

The inn in question turned out to be a gem. Owned by two men who were probably gay but definitely friendly and gourmet cooks at that, it was nestled in a wooded glen along the Appalachian Trail. Though neither of the men had heard of Cyrill Stockland, one of them promptly picked up the phone, called the previous owners and, after a phone call back several hours later, presented us with the name of a private club in Westport, Connecticut, where Cyrill had gone to work when she left the inn.

Tucking that information under our belts, we set about enjoying ourselves for the few remaining hours we had together. We ate dinner by candlelight, sat for a time by the fire in the living room, then retired to our room. It was furnished with authentic antiques, but the only one that truly interested us was the bed. This we utilized for far more active endeavors than sleeping, before finally, reluctantly, succumbing to exhaustion.

In the morning Peter headed for New York while I returned to Maine. As far as friends like Swansy and Cooper were concerned, I had simply been off having a good time with Peter—which was the truth, but not the whole truth. I figured the whole truth was better withheld until I really had it.

I celebrated Thanksgiving as I had for the past six years, with a group of twenty-some-odd friends who congregated at Sam's Saloon. We all chipped in with the cooking, my contribution being two large blueberry jello molds. They were surprisingly delicious given that, in addition to water, there were only three ingredients required.

I was home by dusk. Peter was spending the day with the family of a colleague of his and had promised to call. We had arrangements to make for the weekend, when we were planning to resume our search for the mysterious Cyrill, so I didn't want to miss his call.

At least that was the reason I gave myself for waiting eagerly by the phone. After the call came through, though, after we'd talked and arranged and talked some more, then hung up, I acknowledged that the fullness I felt inside had little to do with Cyrill Stockland.

I didn't question myself further when I left the next morning at the crack of dawn to drive south. Peter and I had agreed that I'd fly to New York and spend Friday night with him at his place, then we'd set out together on Saturday to tackle Westport. But I was too impatient to wait until mid-afternoon for a flight, and since Westport was right on the way, I decided to make a stop.

The manager at the country club had a fascinating story to tell. It seemed that Cyrill Stockland had indeed worked for him and had been quite a hit among his other employees. In fact, when she'd become pregnant, two of them had actually come to blows over which of them had fathered the child. Needless to say, she'd been asked to leave the club. The manager thought he remembered something about her continuing on into New York, but under the circumstances, she'd been given severance pay in cash and hurried out the door. He had no forwarding address. He did, though, still have in his employ one of those men who had fought over her. He had since married another woman and had five children, and the manager wasn't sure whether he'd welcome inquiries about Cyrill Stockland. I managed to persuade him to introduce me nonetheless.

The man in question had moved up in the ranks to become the head groundskeeper of the club. Along with his position must have come a certain amount of self-confidence, because he had no problem thinking back to the days when he'd fought another man for the privilege of claiming the paternity of Cyrill Stockland's child.

"Hoot of it is," he told me, a crooked smile dancing on his round face, "we never even made it together. But I was young and full of myself. And I was damned if the other guy was gonna take the credit. Me and him argued about nearly every woman who stepped foot in the club." He winked at me.

The wink left me cold. As far as I was concerned, there was nothing remotely sexually attractive about the man. He was nowhere near as tall, as well-built, as bright or amusing or compelling as Peter. The sooner I finished with him and went on to New York, the better.

"Did you keep in touch with Cyrill after she left?"

"Nah. Like I say, I had no real stake in it. And she wasn't the kind of girl you kept in touch with. She was ambitious. She was moving on and up, she said, and she had that look about her like she'd really make it one day."

"Do you know where she went?"

"The city."

"New York?"

"That's the one."

"Do you know where in New York?"

He shook his head. "It's a big place. She wanted to get lost while she had the kid, then she figured she'd climb out of her hole and make her fortune."

Cyrill Stockland knew the score. New York was precisely the place to make a fortune, and the place to get lost, which didn't help my search a whole lot. Mildly discouraged, I thanked him for his time. I turned to leave, paused, then turned back. "When did all this happen? If you were to pin down the birth of her child to a particular time, when would it be?"

"I can tell you exactly when it was," the man said without hesitation. "I was here just a year when I got in that fight over her. I know 'cause I nearly blew that first raise I'd been counting on. It was twenty-one years last June when I started here, so she musta had her baby just about twenty years ago."

I hadn't been keeping a particularly close watch on the dates, other than to note that Cyrill hadn't stayed in any one place for long. Now, hearing that she'd given birth to her baby twenty years before, something clicked.

Excited, I thanked the groundskeeper a second time, left and drove into New York. Peter was in conference across town when I arrived at his office; he hadn't expected me until later. I waited patiently at first, then less patiently, until finally he returned.

The look of high pleasure that lit his face when he saw me sitting there was ample compensation for the wait. Kicking his office door closed, he strode across the oriental carpet, put his hands on either arm of my chair, leaned low and captured my mouth. Without touching any other part of me, he made me feel like a million.

He didn't touch any other part of me because he didn't trust himself that far—but he only told me that later, when we were in his apartment with no need for restraint. And we showed none there. Not only were we celebrating our reunion, but with a few phone calls and a little string-pulling on Peter's part, we'd made a major discovery.

"Who'd have thought it?" Peter murmured against my neck. His hands were under my sweater busily working on the buttons of my blouse. "Who'd have guessed Cyrill was Benjie's mom."

I tugged off his tie and dropped it where we stood. "But that's the least of it," I argued as I pulled the tails of his shirt from his trousers. "Cooper's Benjie's dad! Not his half brother. His *dad*!" I slid buttons through holes as quickly as I could. "It was right there on the birth certificate. Clear as day. So why didn't we know? Why didn't anyone say anything?" Pushing the shirt off his shoulders, I had just enough time to press my lips to the hair on his chest when he pulled my sweater over my head.

"Like the people in town?" He tossed the sweater aside and dispensed as quickly with my blouse. "Maybe they didn't know."

"They had to know Cooper's mother wasn't pregnant—help me with this, Peter." I couldn't get his belt undone.

He quickly took care of it. "Not necessarily. If a woman's a little overweight to start with, she could go away for a month and come back with a baby, and the people around her might, just might believe it was hers.'' He'd released the front closing of my bra as quickly as he had his belt. Peeling the lacy cups from my breasts, he tossed the bra aside.

We were both taking short, shallow breaths, as though we'd just come in from a sprint. Our hands tangled from time to time. That slowed us down and increased the impatience.

''I think they knew,'' I decided as I gingerly worked his zipper over his arousal. ''I think they all knew, just kept it to themselves.'' I slipped my hands inside. ''Maybe that's why they were so tolerant— ahhhh, Peter...'' He'd taken half of my breast into his mouth and was drawing on it so strongly that I felt the pull all the way to my womb. Momentarily abandoning the treasure in his briefs, I dug my fingers onto his hair and held on.

''Peter—ahhhhhh—it always comes down to this.'' I gasped when he did something powerful to my nipple with his teeth, then felt instantly bereft when he raised his head.

''Shall I stop?''

''Lord, no!'' I met his mouth in a hungry kiss and slipped my hands back into his briefs. He was hot and hard. The feel of him against my palms sent tiny currents of excitement through my fingers, up my arms and into the rest of my body. I stroked his distended length, taking pride when he grew even more rigid. It seemed that much more and he'd burst—I was feeling the same way inside.

He swore then and, setting me back, went at the rest of my clothes in earnest. ''You distract me so much sometimes,'' he growled, bending on a knee to tug down my skirt and panty hose together, "that I can't concentrate on what I'm doing."

"You were doin' just fine," I teased in a whisper. "You felt just right to hold."

His pale green eyes, shimmering with darker shards and smoldering now, speared me with a hungry gaze. Then he lowered his eyes, leaned forward and kissed me where no one but he had ever kissed me before. It was suitable punishment for my teasing, because I nearly lost it there and then, particularly when his kiss grew deeper, his tongue more aggressive.

"Please!" I cried.

He knew what I wanted. With several rough tugs, he freed me of the last of my clothes, then did the same for himself. For an instant when we were both naked, we just stood there looking at each other's bodies. But our inner demands were insistent. I had to touch him, had to feel the heat of his body on mine, in mine, and it was clear from the urgent way he reached for me that he felt the same.

Our bodies came together in a crush, fitting as perfectly as ever. My arms went around his neck, my legs around his hips when he lifted me, and when I felt the full force of him slide inside, I let out a small cry of pleasure.

To this day, I can't begin to describe that feeling of having Peter inside. It was so many things—fullness, heat, excitement, satisfaction, completion, security—that it boggled my mind.

"Ahhh, Peter," I cried, "what you do to me."

"Tell me," he whispered. "What do I do?"

With his large hands spread under my bottom, he moved his pelvis. I felt him withdraw nearly completely, then slowly, tauntingly return. "You make me burn," I managed to gasp against his neck. "Can't you feel it?"

He didn't answer at first, and when he did, his voice was deep and husky. "I feel it, babe. I feel it." Holding our bodies locked tightly, he carefully lowered me to the bed. Still buried deeply inside me, he held himself up on his arms and looked down into my face.

He was beautiful. His eyes, his face, his body—he was a beautiful person. Tears came to my eyes at the thought of how lucky I was to have him. He made my heart swell to twice its normal size.

His lips touched mine with a gentleness that belied the throbbing I felt inside. "It does always come to this," he said hoarsely, "because this is what I need." He raised his head. His eyes met mine. "It's only when we're together like this that I know you love me."

A knot swelled in my throat to rival the swelling of my heart, and I knew he was right. I hadn't put the word to the emotion I felt, and I didn't want to do it now, but there was no doubt it was real. Nothing else could explain the things he made me feel, even the sense of security I'd thought about moments before. I felt secure when we made love because during those times, Peter was unconditionally mine. I didn't have to share him with anyone or anything. I could touch him and kiss him and hug him and love him. I liked it that way.

With a low moan, he squeezed his eyes shut. "What was that? What did you just do?"

I hadn't realized I'd done anything until my muscles relaxed. "This?" I whispered. I clenched them again.

He made a rough sound, swallowed, nodded. His arms began to tremble. But his eyes, heavy-lidded moments before, grew suddenly large and intense. "I belong here, Jill. I belong inside you, not just when we're making love, but during all the other times, too. You have my heart. You'll always have it. I want yours."

"You have it," I whispered, framing his head with my hands.

"Now. But for always? It's no good if it's only when we're in bed."

I wasn't ready to say the words. Nor could I lie and deny them. So I slipped my hands into his hair and brought his head down to my mouth. Silently I told him how I felt.

It wasn't enough.

Peter lowered himself to his elbows. He held enough of his weight so that I wasn't crushed, but our bodies touched at every possible point. Like the soft, swirling hair on his chest, his voice was a sensual abrader. "I'm insecure about some things, Jill, and you're one." His breath was warm above my face, his eyes hot. "I think about you all the time we're apart, and it eats at me that you may not be thinking about me, too. I need to know you are. I need that commitment. I want you to take the sum of everything that's you, turn it over and endorse it to me. For deposit only. No turning back. No withdrawals. Forever.''

I heard what he said, and part of me wanted just that. I didn't feel threatened; it wasn't a question of losing myself in Peter, as much as being all the richer for a merger with him. But I needed time. I had to come to terms with certain things, and I wasn't about to do that now, not with the sight and scent and feel of him surrounding me.

"Show me what you want," I whispered, and he did. He loved me with everything that was him, and then some, and it was the most glorious feeling in the world. At times he was gentle, at times fierce, making me feel alternatively like a precious jewel and an enchantress. I couldn't say whether I preferred one feeling to another because they were both part of the whole, and the whole captured my mind to such an extent that analysis was impossible.

By the time we fell back to the sheets with our limbs entwined and our skin dewy, though, I knew that there'd never be another love for me like Peter.

We dozed off, awakening after an hour to make love again. After another nap, we awoke ravenous for food of the material kind, but the shower we took first led to a rebirth of passion. It was nearly midnight when Peter opened his front door to two large, loaded pizzas.

Nothing but crumbs remained—Peter ate his own pie, plus three slices of mine—when we took our large, loaded stomachs into the den, wrapped ourselves in each other and a large afghan that Peter had picked up in the course of his travels, and began to talk.

Peter must have known that I wasn't ready to tackle the issue of love and commitment that night, because he bypassed it to talk about Cooper and Cyrill. "Tell me what you think."

I snuggled deeper within the bands of his arms. "I think that Cooper fell hard. He was eighteen, Cyrill seventeen when she came to town. It sounds like she wasn't the type to fall in love. She had plans. But she must have been taken with Cooper, enough to have an affair with him, and the affair went on long after she left Maine."

"Cooper obviously knew when she became pregnant."

"Or learned soon after. He was close enough when the baby was born to claim him and take him home."

"I wonder what kind of deal he had to make."

I tipped my head on his upper arm so that I could see his face. "What do you mean?"

"If Cyrill intended to make it big in New York, the last thing she needed was a baby. I wonder if he had to convince her to go ahead with the pregnancy."

I sucked in a breath. "You think she might have wanted an abortion?"

"Maybe. She sure didn't want the baby, if she allowed him to be taken from her and raised as someone else's child."

My heart ached for Benjie. "Poor kid. Imagine the rejection he's probably felt over the years."

"If he knows the truth."

"I'm sure he does. It would explain the time Benjie

told me in no uncertain words that Cooper would never marry me.''

''All that would explain was Benjie's knowing Cooper's feelings about Cyrill.''

''No. It was more. Benjie's vehemence was exactly like that of a kid being loyal to his mother—or wishing that one day his parents would get back together.''

''It could have just been Benjie's natural raunchiness,'' Peter said.

I was wondering the same thing. Then I shook my head. ''Cooper wouldn't keep something like that from him.'' I paused. ''Would he?''

''I'm the wrong one to be asking. You've known him far longer than I have.''

''But as a man, looking at Cooper, considering your impressions of him, what do you think?''

Peter seemed confused as he looked into my face. ''I'd guess no, but that's all it is, a guess.'' He let out a soft breath. ''But whether Benjie knows the truth or not, the facts of his parentage go a long way in explaining the complexity of Cooper's feelings toward him.''

I returned my cheek to Peter's chest. ''It's so strange—Cooper being Benjie's father. So hard to believe, after all these years.'' But the more I thought about it, the more I realized that it wasn't so hard to believe after all. ''It gives new meaning to lots of things Cooper's said about Benjie.'' For a minute, I was lost in thought. Then, looking up at Peter, I went straight to the heart of the matter. ''Do you think Benjie smuggled those diamonds onto the *Free Reign*?''

"I don't know."

"Do you think Cooper knows?"

Peter arched a brow and shrugged.

I thought of Cooper loving Cyrill and being hurt. I thought of his loving Benjie and being hurt. "Cooper's always been so good. He's always been there for Benjie. But the stakes have never been so high before. It breaks my heart to think of his going to prison for him."

"If he's as innocent as he claims, he's prepared to go to prison for *someone.*"

He fell silent, but something in his words caught in my mind. The same something caught in his mind, too, because I felt the slight pickup of his pulse at the same time that his eyes opened wider. "I wonder."

"Is it possible?"

"Anything's possible."

"Probable, then?"

"If he loved deeply, he'd protect one nearly as staunchly as the other."

"But where is she now?"

"Good question."

"How do we go about finding an answer?" I asked, but Peter was already shifting me on the sofa and rising. Wearing nothing but a pair of sleek navy briefs, he padded around the desk, opened a drawer and removed the Manhattan phone book.

"No Cyrill Stockland," he concluded after he'd run through the list. He removed a second phone book from the drawer and checked, then a third. He wound up with five C. Stocklands, none of whom he could call at one in the morning, and by that time, I'd had enough of looking at the bunching muscles of his shoulders as he leaned over the desk. With the afghan draped shawllike around me, I went to his side and spread the shawl to cover him, too.

Turning to me, he said gently, "We'll find her, babe. Trust me. We'll find her."

He did, though it took four more days and a private investigator to do the trick. But the wait produced a bonus. Cyrill Stockland did, indeed, live in New York, but under the name of Cyrill Kane. Though she hadn't quite made the fortune she'd hoped for twenty years before, she was still trying. She ran with a fast and dubious circle of friends, one of whom was reputed to be a jewel thief.

Even more condemning, one of the investigator's sources had heard rumor that Cyrill and the thief had a new angle that involved Cyrill's "kid."

Peter told me all of this on the phone in the middle of the week, and I nearly went out of my mind with frustration keeping it to myself until he arrived late Friday afternoon. But I couldn't tell Swansy, who already felt guilty for having put us onto Cyrill, and we'd agreed to confront Cooper together.

It was a wise agreement. In all the years I'd known Cooper, he'd never turned as dark as he did when Peter told him about what we'd learned.

Cooper kept his voice low, but there was a palpable tension in it. "I said I didn't want an investigator."

It was a revealing first statement. "You knew?" I asked in a dismayed whisper.

He glared at Peter. "Who told you to hire an investigator?"

"As your lawyer, it was my decision to make."

"I didn't want one."

"That's not the issue," I put in. "Did you know?" Still he didn't confirm or deny what we'd learned. "Cooper?"

The force of his gaze was on Peter. He didn't look at me once. "Can you defend me the way we originally planned?"

"Without mentioning any of this?"

"That's right."

"It's crazy, man."

"Can you do it?"

"Sure, I can do it—"

"You can't!" I broke in.

Peter held up a hand to me. To Cooper, he said, "But it doesn't make any sense. It was one thing when we thought that a total stranger had stashed those diamonds on the boat. But if Benjie is in business with Cyrill, you've got a problem that isn't going away so fast. If you're acquitted, he'll keep at it until he's caught. If you're convicted, he's going to have to live with that. Think he can?"

Cooper's eyes were coal black. "Benjie is innocent."

"Perhaps in the most general sense," Peter said, "but if he was the one who put those diamonds on the *Free Reign*, then stood by and watched you go through hell, somewhere along the line he stops being so innocent."

I felt totally stymied. "Does he know that you know the truth?"

Cooper spared me a glance then. Its harshness was moderated only slightly by the feelings he had for me. As though knowing he couldn't—or didn't dare—sustain any semblance of gentleness for long, he looked back at Peter. "I don't want him touched."

Peter tried to reassure him. "Benjie would be all right. I could get him off with a suspended sentence because of his age and the circumstances—"

"I don't want his name brought into this at all."

"He'd end up with nothing more than probation. It might do him good."

"No."

"Cooper—" I began to protest, but he'd apparently had enough. Storming past us, he whipped his coat from a hook by the door and left with the slam of aged oak.

I looked at Peter. Then I grabbed my own coat from the chair on which I'd dropped it moments before. "I'm going after him."

"Maybe you should give him time to think."

"If I do that, he'll convince himself he's doing the right thing."

"He already has."

"Then my job will be harder, but I have to try."

"I'll come," Peter said.

He was reaching for his coat when I put a hand on his arm. "No. It'd be better if I see him alone." The look in Peter's eyes said that he wasn't so sure about that, but I knew what I was doing. "Cooper and I have something special." I moved my hand to his face and brushed my thumb across his lips. ''It's not what you and I have, but it's still deep. I want to appeal to it, but if you're there, it'll be harder. Cooper will use you to keep me at arm's length.'' I paused. ''I have to try, Peter.''

He didn't move, didn't make any attempt to change my mind. Going up on my toes, I put my mouth where my thumb had been. *I love you,* I thought, and nearly said the words. At the last minute they caught in my throat. I didn't know whether it was the particular circumstance, or whether I just wasn't ready to say them, but by the time I returned my heels to the floor, the moment had passed. I quickly fastened my parka, pulled up my hood and turned toward the front door, only to be stopped by an unexpected sight.

Benjie was standing stiffly in the kitchen doorway.

He had clearly overheard my final conversation with Peter and, just as clearly, had seen me kiss him, but how much he'd heard of what we'd said to Cooper, I didn't know. Nor, at that moment, did I care. Cooper was my main concern. I was very happy to leave Benjie to Peter.

I sent Benjie a look that I hoped was at the same time dignified and imploring, cast a last glance at Peter, then left in search of Cooper.

Dusk was beginning to settle over the coast, bringing with it an increase in the wind and the cold. When I didn't immediately see Cooper on the pier, I huddled more deeply into my coat and headed down Main Street. At the very end, I worked my way down a twisting path that opened onto a small cluster of rocks. Cooper was squatting on one of the larger rocks, tossing pebbles into the frothing sea.

I continued on down until I stood close behind him. Without turning, he knew I'd come. No doubt he'd been expecting me.

His voice rose above the tumult of the tides. "It won't work, Jill. You can talk until you're blue in the face, but I'm not changing my mind. I don't want Benjie involved, and that's that. The issue is closed."

I opened my mouth to launch into my arguments anyway, then closed it again and rethought what I wanted to say. Cooper glanced at me. Pressing my fists deep into my pockets, I came down on my haunches by his side so I wouldn't have to shout.

"Tell me about her, Cooper. Tell me what she was like."

He shot me another glance, this time in mild surprise. Then he tossed a few more pebbles into the sea, and just when I was beginning to wonder whether he'd answer, he began to speak quietly. "She was beautiful. Tall, blond, curvy in all the right places. The first time I saw her, I felt like I'd been hit. Knocked the air right out of me."

I certainly knew what that was like, but I'd never imagined Cooper being susceptible to lightning like that. "Love at first sight?"

He shrugged. "I was just a kid. The only girls I'd known were the ones around here, and they weren't satisfying me when I needed it." He took a breath. "She was younger than me, but more experienced. One night with her, and I was hooked."

I wanted to ask why he hadn't married her and kept

her here, but I already knew the answer. Cyrill wasn't slowing down for anyone. "How long did it go on?"

"We were together the whole time she was here. I followed her a couple of other places. Then she went to New York. She was always straight about that. She told me she'd never marry me. She didn't want the boonies, and she didn't want me, but she had my baby, and I wanted him. He was a little bit of her."

He was a lot of her, I was thinking sadly. "Have you seen her since Benjie was born?"

He shook his head.

"Did you try?"

Again he shook his head. He tossed another pebble into the surf, then said in a voice so small that I nearly missed it, "I was afraid."

"That she'd turn you away?"

After a bit he shrugged. "She knows where I am. She knows I'd take her if she just said the word."

That was what was so hard for me to understand. The Cooper I'd know, respected, loved was an independent and pragmatic man. I had trouble conceiving of his being a slave to a woman, particularly one who wasn't worthy of him. "You'd do that, even after all this time?"

He pushed out his lips, thought a minute, nodded. "I still dream about her."

I could bet she was the one on his mind when he slaked his physical needs on other women. "Do you still love her?"

He took up another pebble, rubbed it against the larger rock for a minute before tossing it away. "Yes, I still love her," he admitted angrily. "And don't ask me to explain it. But there's a certain feeling. It comes every time I think of her. Call it an obsession if you want, I'm sure it's that, but I can't stop it.''

He tossed his pebbles with greater passion. I wondered whether he got relief doing that and contemplated trying it out. I was feeling very frustrated.

''Tell me what it's like, Cooper. Tell me what it's like to love someone so much that you'd sacrifice your entire future for her.''

He cast me a sharp sidelong glance. ''I don't have to tell you. You're the expert on the subject.''

My heart skipped a beat. ''What do you mean?''

''You and Adam. You're sacrificing your future for him.''

''I am not.''

''You are, and he's not even around to see. At least in my case I'll know that Cyrill is free because of what I've done.''

''That doesn't make *sense*.''

''It does to me, and that's all that counts.''

''But she wouldn't do the same for you.''

''Neither would Adam for you.''

''Obviously not, since he's dead.''

''He wouldn't have done it if he'd been alive. And if the tables had been turned, he *sure* wouldn't have done it. If you'd been the one to have an accident and die, he'd have been out of here like a shot, and he'd never have come back.''

Swansy had said nearly the same thing not so long before. I hadn't wanted to hear it then, and I didn't want to hear it now. ''Why are you saying this, Cooper? You and Adam were so close!''

"Yes, we were." He swiveled on the balls of his feet to face me more fully. "But I wasn't in love with him, so I could see him more clearly than you could. He had a whole lot of strong points, but none of them had to do with this kind of life. And you knew it. You knew it wasn't working, and you might have done something about it, but then he upped and died, so it was too late." He barely paused for a breath. "You've spent the last six years idealizing him, Jill. You felt guilty about his death, so you made yourself a living memorial to him."

I stood quickly. "That's not true—"

"It is," he argued right back as he, too, straightened. His face was shadowed by the oncoming night, but I could sense the tightness of his expression. "You've refused to think anything negative about him. You've pushed your love to a place where it probably never was, and because of that, you're holding back on Peter, even though he's just right for you. So if you want to talk about sacrificing futures, *you* tell *me*."

"You're wrong."

"I don't think so. I know you, Jill. I can see how you relate to Peter, and you haven't related that way to any other person here, including Adam. You look up to Peter. He excites you. You come alive when you're with him. He challenges you. Maybe he frightens you for the same reasons, because for years now you've been with people who don't challenge you at all, and that's easy. It's comfortable. And it's everything you didn't have when you were growing up, but there has to be a middle of the road somewhere. You can't close yourself off and take the easy way out for the rest of your life.''

I put my hands to my ears, shook my head and turned to leave, but Cooper caught my arm. ''Think about it, Jill.''

''There's nothing to think about. And how did we get off on me, anyway? We're supposed to be talking about you!''

''But you're the issue. Your life is the one that can be changed.'' He tightened his grip on my arm, dipped his head a bit and spoke more urgently. ''Don't you see, Jill? I'm a lost cause. I'm stuck in whatever kind of bind this is, and as long as Cyrill is alive, and as long as Benjie's her son, I'll be the way I am. No other woman I've met gives me the kind of feeling she gave me, so if I settled for another woman, I'd be settling for second best. What kind of woman wants to be second best?''

He had his answer when I remained silent.

''So forget saving me,'' he said. ''I'm too old to change.''

''You're not too old. You're too bull-headed.''

''And you? Are you too different?''

''Yes!''

''Doesn't look it from where I stand.''

''I'm just being careful. I don't want to rush into anything.''

''Well, let me tell you, sweetheart, you go on clinging to Adam and see where it gets you. It's gonna get you nowhere. *Nowhere.*''

''I don't have to listen to this,'' I muttered. Wrenching my arm from his grasp, I ran back up the path. It was darker now. I stumbled once or twice and felt Cooper reach for me. Each time, though, I caught my balance and ran ahead. When I reached the street, I walked as quickly as I could toward the north end of town.

"Don't blow it, Jill!" Cooper yelled from somewhere behind me.

"Why not?" I yelled back. "You've done it. Why can't I do it, too?"

"Because," he said, keeping pace with me from one step back, "lonely is a lousy way to live. If another woman had come along to knock me in the gut the way Cyrill did, I'd have grabbed her fast. But no one ever came."

"What does that have to do with me?"

"You've got Peter."

I stopped dead cold and faced him with my hands on my hips. "And you think that what I have with Peter matches what I had with Adam? You've got a hell of a lot of nerve assuming that." Before he could respond, I whirled around and strode quickly down the street again.

Moments later he caught my hand and stopped me again. His voice was deep and oddly gentle as it came through the darkness and the cold. "You mean a lot to me, Jill. We've been friends since you moved here, and I've valued that. There have been times since Adam died when I thought I was crazy not to stir something up with you. Not that you'd have gone for it, but it might have been worth a try if only to keep you here as my friend forever. Only I can't do it. You deserve more—more than I can give you, more than any man around here can give you. I don't much like the idea of your leaving, but you need broader spaces—"

"I'm not going anywhere."

"You will. You love him."

"I'm not *going anywhere.*"

Rather than contradict me again, Cooper wrapped his arms around me and drew me close. I was so surprised by the gesture, coming from him, that I didn't protest. I had the feeling that he was telling me without words how much he meant all he'd said.

We didn't stand there for long—it couldn't have been more than ten seconds—before he held me back and looked down into my face. The faint glow from the Prentiss's front light post gave his eyes a liquid sheen. I knew it had to be the light; Cooper would never cry. He was too strong, too controlled. Still, the thought of it held as much meaning as his hug had.

Together we turned and walked on down the street. We hadn't gone more than five or six paces when first Cooper, and then I, stopped again. Standing a dozen yards ahead, at the point where the pier joined Main Street, stood Peter and Benjie.

Intuitively I knew they'd made a deal.

10

I was feeling very much alone. Peter had left me that way in what was probably one of the shrewdest non-legal moves he'd ever made.

He'd made his share of shrewd legal moves, too, before he returned to New York. It seemed that Benjie had overheard most everything we'd said to Cooper, and though he'd known the truth about Cyrill for years, something in Cooper's manner had touched him. That seemed miraculous to me, seeing as I'd always thought Benjie to be such a dyed-in-the-wool brat, though I supposed he had to inherit a *little* of Cooper's character.

At any rate, Benjie had decided on his own, it turned out, with the barest encouragement from Peter, that Cooper deserved more than he'd gotten. At that point Peter's expertise came into play. He made the appropriate phone calls, met with the appropriate officials and took Benjie into Portland when the wheels of justice shifted into gear. He maneuvered U.S. Attorney Hummel so deftly that Benjie was all but guaranteed a suspended sentence based on his testimony against the others.

That testimony was a sore point, since it meant pointing a finger at Cyrill. Again, Peter came through for us. Through a bit of clever arguing, before Cyrill's name was ever introduced, he managed to extract a promise from Hummel that she would be given leniency if she, in turn, agreed to testify against the mastermind of the plot. According to Benjie, this man had used them both. We all knew that Cyrill could well blow it all by refusing to cooperate when she was apprehended, but at least the road was paved for her to have an easier time.

Though the charges against Cooper were dropped, he wasn't thrilled with the goings-on. His brain told him that what had happened was for the best. His heart wasn't as cooperative. Instead of simply fretting about himself now, he fretted about Benjie and Cyrill. He wanted to be able to do something, but there was nothing to be done. Though he had his boat back and his ability to work, he felt more upended than before.

So I couldn't go crying on Cooper's shoulder when Peter returned to New York without me. I couldn't cry on Swansy's shoulder, because she'd become less than sympathetic to my plight. Nor could I cry on the shoulders of any of my friends in town; that just wasn't my role in their eyes.

Time and again, I wondered why Peter hadn't confronted me before he'd left. He knew that there would be no legal reason for him to return to the coast before the trial, which would now be at least four or five months off. And it wasn't as if I had another show coming up soon in New York. Nor was it as if we'd had a fight or anything. We were as close as ever. We had moments of explosive passion and moments of quiet camaraderie. He continued to tell me he loved me, and he did it often.

But he didn't ask whether I loved him back. He didn't demand to hear the words. He didn't ask what I was doing with the rest of my life. He didn't even ask what I was doing with the rest of my week.

At least he hadn't left with a dumb, "See ya." And he did call, I have to stay that. He phoned me every evening at seven-thirty or eight, almost as though he was coming home to me after a long day's work. He'd ask how my day had been and what I'd done. I'd ask about his. But we didn't make plans to see each other.

He was calling my bluff. He was sitting back there in New York waiting for me to do something. I can't say that he was waiting smugly, because deep inside, Peter wasn't that kind of person. I had the feeling that he was truly nervous that I'd decide to live out the rest of my life in solitude on the coast of Maine.

Certainly the solitude he'd afforded me gave me time to think, and I did that with the brutal honesty that I'd avoided before. Given Peter's retreat and the fact that if I didn't do something I could well lose him, I knew that I couldn't keep on playing the games I had. Indeed, the time for brutal honesty had come.

I loved Peter. I'd known it for some time, but now I faced it head-on. I thought of how wonderful I felt when we were together. Cooper was right; I did come alive when I was with Peter. He excited me. He made me feel intelligent and attractive, feminine, cherished, protected. He made me feel that I could face the entire world—and then my family—with my chin held high. He even made me feel sexier than Samantha.

Mostly, though, there was that feeling of wholeness, which I'd never known before.

Adam hadn't made me feel whole. I spent a lot of time thinking about that. Adam was handsome and honest and gentle. He had a great voice and stars in his eyes, and I loved him very much at that time in my life. But it was as though he was an adjunct of me. Swansy had laid it out right; I was the stronger of the two of us. I was the one who carried the emotional weight, as well as the material, if the truth were told.

Facing my guilt was something else. I spent hours shivering on the bluff in the freezing cold, looking out to sea, trying to communicate with Adam. I wanted him to know that whatever I'd done I'd done with the best of intentions. If I'd been blind to his needs or wants in my own drive for independence from my family, I was sorry. The last thing I'd ever wanted was for him to be hurt.

For so many hours I concentrated, looking out to sea that way. And I kept waiting to feel his forgiveness, but it never came. Adam was dead and gone. For the first time I accepted the finality of it. And with that acceptance came the realization that the forgiveness I sought had to come from myself.

In time it did come—largely with the realization that what I felt for Peter didn't detract from the memory of what I'd felt for Adam. I loved both men, Adam, then, Peter now, and I loved them in very different ways. Adam was an important part of my past. Peter was my future.

Increasingly I began to dream about the future. I

dreamed about keeping my place on the shore and Peter's place in the city, and maybe even buying a country place in between. I dreamed about taking trips with Peter to the far-off and unusual places he favored. I even let myself go and dreamed about having children. Peter's children. It was a...heart-catching thought.

I think what finally did it, though, was that Monday noontime at Swansy's. I hadn't seen Peter in two weeks, and two long, lonely weeks they'd been. I'd just come off another weekend with seemingly everyone doing fun things but me, and when I arrived at Swansy's, she was listening to her soap.

I stood there with my eyes glued to the television set, watching a kaleidoscope of human drama. In the space of thirty minutes, I heard mention of birth, death, feast, famine, crime, adventure and mischief. I felt like a voyeur, like a fly on the wall of life, and it struck me that that wasn't the way I wanted to live. I wanted to do things, to experience life firsthand, well beyond the scope of my potting. And I wanted to do all that with Peter.

After two weeks alone, time was suddenly of the essence. Without a word of explanation, I gave Swansy a long, tight hug. Then I rushed home, changed clothes, packed a light bag and drove to the airport.

I was in New York by five. Knowing that Peter would still be at the office, I taxied to his place on Central Park South. The attendant didn't know me. He wouldn't let me up without Peter, but that was fine. I was here. I could wait.

That was just what I did for three hours until finally he returned from the office. I was sitting in the lobby watching the door when he came into sight. I stood quickly, then folded my hands in front of me and waited.

Our eyes met. My heart did the same catching number that I was sure it would do for Peter until the day I died. Slowly and with deliberate steps, I walked over to where he stood.

"I didn't know you were here," he said a little apologetically, a little cautiously. "Have you been waiting long?"

I nodded. "The time was good, though." I felt a tiny smile escape. "It gave me a chance to back out."

Something like hope flared in his wonderfully luminescent green eyes, and only at that instant did it hit me that I had never once doubted he'd want me. I had never feared he'd change his mind. It was a tribute to the way I trusted him, to the way I trusted his love.

When he continued to eye me with a very cautious hope, it occurred to me that he hadn't been as sure of me. He still didn't know what my verdict was. It wasn't that he trusted me any less than I trusted him, but that not once had I told him in words how I felt.

It was time. I raised a hand to his cheek, then slid it down and grasped the lapel of his topcoat. "I do love you, Peter."

The hope in his eyes became less cautious and more sure, but it was still only hope. "What is it you want?" he asked in a whisper, as though he was almost afraid to say the words at all, let alone aloud, lest he didn't like the answer. I understood. For all he knew, I could love him but not be willing to make the commitment he craved.

"I want," I said taking a deep breath, "years and years of things like afternoons at the museum and weekends at the shore, long nights of loving and breakfasts in bed. I want a very small wedding, a house in the country with a studio out back, and two or three or four kids, or as many as is necessary until we get at least one of each sex."

"One of each, eh?" he asked, grinning now and pleased enough with my proposition to slide his arms around my waist.

I nodded. "I want a little boy to carry on the best of you, and a little girl to carry on the best of me. I think we're both pretty special."

His grin widened. "Y'do?"

I nodded, but I'd had enough of cuteness. My expression sobered. "I want us to be together always, Peter. I've felt only half-whole these past two weeks. I can live with making that deposit you wanted as long as you stick around to fill the void." I paused for the beat of my heart. "Will you?"

The look on Peter's face was so rich with love that he didn't have to answer. But he did it anyway. "Will I ever," he said with such feeling that I burst out laughing. It was a laugh of pure happiness, the first of many, many to come.